VALLEY OF BRAVE HEARTS

Living in an isolated static caravan in the Lake District would seem to be the ideal solution to mend Judith's broken heart and get her life back on track. However, Fate intervenes in the shape of unforeseen disasters. Her only recourse is to seek help from a local matchmaking teenager and his reluctant, embittered and widowed father. The fact that the man is also a vet *and* the local hero just complicates matters further . . .

JUNE GADSBY

VALLEY OF BRAVE HEARTS

Complete and Unabridged

LINFORD
Leicester

First published in Great Britain in 2007

First Linford Edition
published 2008

British Library CIP Data

Gadsby, June
   Valley of brave hearts.—Large print ed.—
Linford romance library
   1. Lake District (England)—Fiction
   2. Love stories 3. Large type books
   I. Title
   823.9'2 [F]

   ISBN 978–1–84782–222–2

Published by
F. A. Thorpe (Publishing)
Anstey, Leicestershire

Set by Words & Graphics Ltd.
Anstey, Leicestershire
Printed and bound in Great Britain by
T. J. International Ltd., Padstow, Cornwall

This book is printed on acid-free paper

1

'Spare a quid for a cuppa, missus?' Judith didn't know where the old tramp had come from, but suddenly he was there on the path in front of her, barring her way.

'I never carry money,' she told him sharply and Bertie gave a low warning growl, pulling back a menacing upper lip.

The tramp raised a shaggy eyebrow at the dog. 'Nasty-looking mutt ye've got there,' he said.

'He can get even nastier if he has to,' Judith told him, upset by the insult to her companion of fifteen years.

On cue, Bertie's growl became louder and even more menacing than the thunder that was rolling around the Lakeland valley. The teeth he showed were white and sharp and she knew that he would use them if he thought she was being threatened.

'Damn stupid dog, that, wi' only three legs. Bet ye I could outrun 'im.'

'Then you'd lose your bet.'

Judith was determined not to show fear, even though her heart was palpitating because of this unpleasant individual, which she could smell across the short distance separating them.

Before things had a chance to get nasty, a jeep came trundling along the rough track and skidded to a halt, spraying muddy water everywhere, but especially on Judith and Bertie.

'Is there a problem here?'

The deep voice boomed from inside the jeep, but it was the youthful passenger, a boy of about seventeen, who alighted. He took in the situation, hands on slim hips, eyes regarding her with open curiosity.

'Is that your Citroen C3 in the ditch back there?' Not the same as the first voice, but it had a similar timbre.

'Yes. I skidded on some mud . . . ' she said, glancing pointedly down at her mud-drenched skirt that had been caused by their jeep more than her landing in a ditch.

'Sorry about that,' the boy apologised with an embarrassed grimace.

'I suppose it couldn't be helped,' she said.

Judith's embarrassed gaze wandered to the driver of the jeep, who was keeping a low profile. No doubt he had a disliking for helpless females, and didn't appreciate them wasting his time.

She wasn't all that helpless, she argued silently in her own defence. Except, of course, when it came to getting cars out of deep mud in torrential rain.

The tramp gave them one last stare, then wandered away, grumbling to himself.

There was a muttered conversation between the two jeep men that she couldn't make out because of the howling wind and driving rain. The boy turned to her again. He was a

3

good-looking kid with friendly eyes and probably set all the girls' hearts aflutter with just one glance.

'Take no notice of Fred,' he said, nodding in the direction of the tramp's retreating back. 'He's harmless. Hop in and we'll give you a lift.'

Judith looked uncertainly at him and at the silent driver of the jeep, who seemed to be doing his best to ignore her.

'It's all right. I have a static caravan not far from here. It's just my luck that the storm broke before I got there.'

'We get a lot of storms in this valley. I bet it was a bit of a shock, skidding into the ditch like that.' The boy grinned. 'I'm Ben Telford, by the way. And the old grump at the wheel is my dad.'

Ben was fondling her dog's silky ears and Bertie was actually trying to shove his nose into the lad's hand, which was unusual. He was normally mistrustful of strangers.

There was a sharp word from the

driver of the jeep, masked by a loud burst of thunder. The boy responded with a few impatient words, then he shrugged his shoulders and turned back to Judith.

'Come on. We can take you as long as you don't mind calling at the Barrett farm first,' he said.

'Oh, I wouldn't want to put you out,' Judith told him, feeling ridiculous standing there in the rain, loaded down with her luggage, water running in rivulets down her face and dripping from her nose and chin.

'Look, would you please stop dithering, woman, and get in before you drown!' The brusque command came from the dim interior of the jeep.

Without further ado, Ben grabbed her holdalls and threw them aboard, as if he were well used to making decisions for other people. He gave her and Bertie a helping hand to mount into the back passenger seat and before she could catch her breath the jeep started off with a disgruntled roar, shooting up great fountains of mud in its wake.

'Don't mind my father,' Ben smiled at her over his shoulder as they drove off up the hill with an angry crunch of gears. 'He's not known for his good manners, but he's the best vet for miles around . . . '

'Which is why I'm in a blessed hurry right now,' the driver of the vehicle ground out and threw her a hasty look in the rear view mirror. 'I have an urgent call to make. A prize bull with a bad case of pneumonia. Where's this caravan of yours, then?'

Judith's eyes met his for the first time in the mirror. They were dark and brooding and she decided that she might have been better off walking after all, despite the storm. However, a pathetic whimper from Bertie, sitting beside her, giving off that particular wet-dog odour, changed her mind. Like most animals, Bertie was scared of storms. He wasn't the only one.

'It's on the hill overlooking Merrivale,'

she told him, wincing as a flash of fork lightning sliced through the darkening sky on the road ahead.

'I know the place, Dad!' Ben exclaimed and looked at her for confirmation. 'Isn't it called Rose Cottage?'

Judith laughed and nodded. Her friends had bought the static van as a holiday home not long after they had married. George and Maggie had lovingly turned the surrounding land, which they also owned, into a perfumed English garden and there were even roses climbing around the door. She had spent a weekend there once and found it idyllic. But that was before Tom; before they got married — and before the divorce.

'Are you here on holiday, then?' It was Ben who asked; his father seemed too distracted to even try to be sociable. But then, he did have a sick bull to visit, Judith thought, trying to find an excuse for his lack of courtesy.

'Sort of,' she told them hesitantly, not

wishing to enter into the reason behind her visit. 'A long break. I needed to . . . to get away. I'm renting Rose Cottage for a few months.'

'Genial!' The boy sounded unusually enthusiastic and she guessed that he was that way by nature, unlike his morose father.

She looked up to find that the dark, fathomless eyes of the vet were again upon her. They were such penetrating eyes. Judith gave an involuntary shudder and put a comforting arm about Bertie. The dog grunted a response and shuffled closer, pressing himself against her side.

'How did your dog lose his leg?'

She looked up, surprised he had noticed. Bertie had been an expert at managing on three legs for a number of years now. Until recently, he could still outrun any of his canine counterparts. However, old age was finally catching up with him.

'It was a tumour,' she said. 'It started in his paw and worked its way up until the vet thought it would be better to amputate.'

'He must have been a nice-looking dog in his heyday.'

'He's still beautiful to me,' she said warmly and felt his eyes on her again. He was probably mocking her for getting all soppy over a bedraggled old mongrel with only three legs. She wished he would simply ignore her and concentrate on the driving.

The jeep swerved off the rough road on to an even rougher track, skidding and squelching through watery ruts, bouncing over tree roots and stones.

'Here we are. You'd better come in. I don't know how long this is going to take.'

'Oh, no, really, Mr . . . um . . . ' Damn! She had forgotten his name. 'I don't want to put you out any more than I have to . . . '

'Nonsense! I don't want to have to think about you sitting out here in the storm while I'm trying to do my job. That would be too distracting. Bring the dog, too, but keep him on a tight leash. There are new lambs.'

He switched off the engine and the jeep shuddered into silence. When he got out and strode off around the back of the rambling old farmhouse, Judith couldn't help noticing his height and his powerful build. His waterproof was voluminous, but there were broad shoulders and muscles lurking beneath it that were impressive even in the growing darkness.

'He's had a bad day,' Ben said apologetically. 'It's been nothing but bad news since early this morning. Dad doesn't like losing animals.'

Judith pulled her anorak around her as she hurried with the boy towards the farmhouse. 'Don't tell me he's really a big softie at heart?'

She didn't mean it to come out quite so sarcastically, but when she saw Ben's expression, she knew her words had struck him like barbs.

'If you knew him, you wouldn't have said that,' he told her, his forehead creasing into a frown. 'Everybody around here likes Rory Telford. He's their hero. Mine too.'

Maybe it was the shock of the accident, the unexpected encounter with the tramp, or the storm — Judith didn't know, but she felt depressed and irritable and here was this nice boy defending his most aloof and surly father and it irked.

'Well, I'm sorry, but I really thought his behaviour was uncalled for,' she said as he pushed open the big front door and called out to someone inside. 'Look, I'm obviously in the way here, so if you can point me in the right direction, I'll find my own way to Rose Cottage and leave you and your father in peace.'

Ben looked perturbed. He shyly touched her hand, then turned to Bertie and gave the dog's head a caress.

'Don't be silly! It's miles to Rose Cottage. You'll drown. Besides, we have to pass that way to get home.'

'Well, I . . . '

Too late to make a decision. A stout, rosy-cheeked woman in a floral wrap-around apron came stomping down the hall towards a them, a beaming smile of welcome lighting up her jovial face.

'Well, look at you, m'dear!' The woman took Judith's arm and led her into a firelit living-room where the air was filled with the tantalising smell of freshly-baked bread and meat stew. 'Rory said he'd picked up a waif and stray on the road here. Bless you! You're soaked to the skin, you and your poor wee dog. Here, my loves, come and sit by the fire until Rory is finished with Samson.'

'You're so kind, but I don't want to be a nuisance . . . '

'Get away with ye, lassie! Any friend of Rory Telford's is a friend of ours and most welcome.'

'Oh, but . . . '

'Not another word, now. I'll make us a pot of tea — and no doubt you, Ben, will be wantin' a hot cheese scone or two, eh?'

Ben nodded happily. 'I was hoping, Mrs Barrett.'

'I thought you might, so I baked some specially for ye, as soon as I knew ye were comin'.' The woman then frowned at Ben. 'He's not lookin' so good th' day, laddie. But then, it's a bad time for the poor man, being as how it's the anniversary.'

'Yeah, and it seems like everything's gone wrong today too.'

'Ach, that doesn't help. Well I'll just go and fetch those scones. They're still warm from the oven. Ye'll want butter on them too? Course ye will!'

Having answered her own question, she hurried off, humming a cheerful tune, her rounded hips undulating with every rolling step. Ben turned a smiling face on Judith, who was hugging the fire and trying not to shiver.

'Mrs Barrett makes the best scones and cakes in the world,' he told her.

'That's quite a recommendation,' she smiled back.

'She's a super person. She was very

good to us when Mum got too sick to look after herself.'

'That's when you find out who your friends are, Ben,' Judith said. 'I hope your mother has recovered now.'

Ben flinched and his tongue flicked out over his lips. She saw immediately the sadness that crept into the boy's dark eyes, eyes so like his father's.

'Mum died ten years ago — ten years today, actually. That's why Dad's in a bit of a mood. He looked after her for years while she was sick, but they couldn't save her. Mum was very brave, but she just wasted away and he never got over it.'

'Oh, Ben, I'm so sorry.'

'You weren't to know, but now maybe you can understand why he was a bit offhand with you. He never used to be like that. He was always laughing and joking — you know — enjoying life. I don't remember much before Mum got ill — I was very young. But people are always telling me that they were an ideal couple.'

'Aye, they were an' all,' Mrs Barrett rattled through the doorway carrying a well-stocked tea tray and set it down before them. 'We all hope he'll find someone else. Lord knows he deserves some happiness after what he's been through, but . . . '

The woman raised her eyebrows and shrugged.

'Well, maybe one day . . . ' Judith ventured, but her words received a definite shake of the head.

'Rory Telford is the most stubborn man you could ever wish to meet, m'dear. He says there'll never be another for him, ever, and when he gets that look on him, we all know he'll not be budged, come hell or high water. Isn't that so, Ben?'

Ben pulled a face and nodded, then the scrape of a shoe on the stone flooring in the hall made them all look up. Rory Telford was still frowning, but looking more relaxed as he joined them, his urgent task completed.

'I'm happy to announce that Samson

will live to sire a lot more little bulls and heifers,' he said, the suspicion of an attractive smile lighting up his strong face.

'Well, that's good news indeed,' Mrs Barrett heaved a sigh of relief. 'Now, sit you down and relax for a wee while.'

'She's baked us some cheese scones, Dad,' Ben told his father, whose face broke into a real smile, shedding years.

'In that case, Mrs Robbins' kittens can wait.' He glanced across at Judith. 'I don't suppose you fancy taking on a kitten or two at Rose Cottage? I've been asked to find homes for six of the little blighters — again. The woman refuses to have her cat spayed then she doesn't want to know when the poor animal gives birth like shelling peas three or four times a year. I've even offered to do the operation free, but she says it's not natural and that's that.'

Judith wondered why he was staring at her so unexpectedly, then realised that he had asked her a question which she hadn't responded to — for the simple reason that she was finding the grumpy driver of the jeep far too attractive for her own good.

'I would love a kitten, Dr Telford,' she said, a warm flush spreading through her. 'Unfortunately, Bertie wouldn't agree.'

At the sound of his name, the dog raised his head, waggled a pair of large ears and gave a soft moan. The vet leaned over and gave him a stroke.

'Yes, I suppose he's too old to learn new tricks. OK, son, no kittens. You deserve to live out the rest of your days without stress.'

'Unlike some I could mention, who are far too young to be resting on their laurels,' Mrs Barrett said, exchanging a secret smile with Ben that made Judith feel particularly left out.

'Maybe Bertie would like a nice lady dog,' Mrs Barrett said with a sly wink, 'Unless he's too set in his ways, like some people I know.'

'Who would that be?' Rory Telford scowled good-naturedly and reached for a butter-drenched scone.

Mrs Barrett and Ben exchanged knowing glances and laughed, the complicity between them strong. The vet's gaze fleetingly met Judith's, then slid away.

2

They didn't spend long over Mrs Barrett's tea and scones, delicious though they were. The vet was obviously on edge and he got noticeably irritable with his son on a couple of occasions, for no apparent reason. Ben, fortunately, was a good-natured lad and it seemed to wash over him like a wavelet breaking on a beach. In fact, Judith thought, Ben seemed to find his father's irascibility highly amusing.

'You'd be sure to look in on me, m'dear,' Mrs Barrett said as she saw them out. 'It's pretty isolated up where you're going. A person can get good and lonely with only her own voice to listen to.'

Judith thanked the woman for her kindness, secretly thinking that it would be some time before she got tired of her own company. After all, the whole idea of her being in George and Maggie's caravan was to get away from people, and life in general.

Out of the corner of her eye, she caught Ben giving his father a nudge. 'We'll invite you round for Sunday lunch, eh, Dad?'

The boy was grinning enthusiastically, but Rory Telford looked uncomfortable. It had obviously been the wrong thing to suggest.

'I'm sure Judith has better things to do with her time,' Rory said as he urged them back down the path to the waiting jeep.

Ben shrugged off his father's rebuff with a laugh. 'He's only saying that because he's a pretty hopeless cook. On the other hand, I cook a great Sunday joint. I'm hoping to be a chef, so it'd be great to have someone to practice on. Other than Dad, that is. He doesn't appreciate my *haute cuisine*.'

There was a short grunt of displeasure from Rory, who was already concentrating heavily on the driving, for which Judith was glad. The storm had gathered force and was whipping across the hillsides, bending the trees in its path.

'It's an offer I might take you up on one day, Ben,' she said, having to raise her voice above the rattle of thunder. 'But for the moment I plan to enjoy being something of a hermit.'

'That's not much fun,' Ben threw back at her.

'Now, Ben, stop that,' his father gave him a sharp look, then turned it on Judith for an instant before the winding road ahead reclaimed his attention. 'It's time you learnt to respect the decisions of others.'

'If you ask me, you two hermits would get on like a house on fire . . . ' He stopped short and twisted around to face her. 'Oh, you're not married or anything, are you, Judith?'

Automatically, she rubbed her thumb on the finger where her wedding and engagement rings had been. It was now void of jewellery, though there was an unmistakable indentation where they had been.

'I'm divorced,' she said, muttering it in a short, throwaway line.

Ben didn't say any more, but smiled at her broadly before looking at his father. Rory's eyes were fixed straight ahead. Not another word was spoken until they slithered to a halt at the perimeter fence bearing the sign, *Rose Cottage*.

'Help Judith with her luggage,' Rory told his son, ignoring the frown he received in return. 'Go on. It's late and we're all tired.'

'I can manage, really!' Judith said, anxious to have time to herself.

'Don't you think we should go in with her, Dad?' Ben asked. 'You know, make sure everything's OK? It's been standing empty for ages.'

It was true that Maggie and George no longer used the place for their holidays. They were getting on and preferred the luxury of hotels in warmer climes. However, they had assured her that all services had been arranged ahead of her arrival.

Before she could say anything, however, Rory was out of the jeep and marching up the path in front of them, his flashlight illuminating the long white static van with its blue-painted door and the bright green spring leaves of the climbing roses that surrounded it.

'Really, it's very kind of you, but I'm sure everything's all right.'

'No, Ben's right. It is best to check, then we'll leave you in peace.'

The words were thrown carelessly over his shoulder, but she got the distinct impression that there was an edginess in his tone.

The first thing they noticed was a broken window. And a sudden gust of wind showed them that the door was open, swinging drunkenly on its hinges. Judith's heart plummeted.

'Looks like a break-in,' Ben said.

Rory was already inside, the flashlight swinging everywhere. They heard an expression of disgust and a cough.

'Don't come in here!' he shouted and came out so quickly he collided with Judith and had to grab hold of her before she toppled over.

'What's wrong?'

He set her firmly to one side and released his grip, which had been so strong she felt bruised by it.

'Somebody's been dossing down in there. Old Fred, no doubt. Anyway, it's pretty disgusting and there's no electricity. The storm's probably responsible for that.'

'Aagh!' Ben, who needed to see the scene of the crime for himself, pulled his head back sharply. 'You can't stay there, Judith. Can she, Dad?'

'No, she can't.' Rory stood looking about him. 'Unfortunately, the inn in the village is closed for repairs . . . '

'Well, I don't seem to have any choice,' Judith said grimly, trying to suppress a rising wave of panic at the thought of being alone in a vandalised caravan without electricity, and no car.

This trip had been planned to get her life back on track after a difficult marriage and a messy divorce. When Maggie suggested that she spend some time recharging her batteries at *Rose Cottage* it had seemed the perfect solution.

'She can stay with us, Dad,' Ben turned to Judith with an optimistic smile. 'We've got a spare bedroom.'

'Oh, no! Really, I couldn't ... ' Judith started to object, but neither of her companions was listening.

'Come on — back in the jeep.' Rory had taken one of Judith's bags and was striding off with it. 'We can't leave you out here like this. Come on. I haven't time to listen to all that feminine pride. Come along, woman, before you sink up to your knees in the mud.'

Judith heard a boyish snigger in her ear and then Ben was gripping her arm as manfully as his father had done, marching her back to the jeep.

'See, I told you he was all right,' the boy said. 'I hope you like *daube de boeuf au vin rouge*, because that's what I'm making for supper tonight.'

'In other words, beef stew,' Rory said, but managed a smile that told her he wasn't entirely indifferent to his son's passion for cooking. 'And Jamie Oliver here has used a whole bottle of my best wine.'

It sounded fine to Judith and she said so, but she wasn't sure how she was going to like being a houseguest in the home of a somewhat reluctant host, even if he was a local hero.

3

'Right, that's got that sorted.' Roy had spent the last half-hour on the phone talking to the police and one or two other people in order to get cleaning and repairs started on the van. Meanwhile, Judith had enjoyed the luxury of a hot bath and a change of clothes.

'I'm so grateful,' she said with genuine sincerity, having decided that the Telfords, father and son, were bona fide and not people to mistrust.

She was still feeling a little stunned, not quite believing that she was here in this cosy stone cottage, boarding with a surly stranger and his surprisingly friendly son. Her friends and family would be amazed to hear of it, but short of sitting out the storm in a wrecked static van, there hadn't been much else she could have done.

'Joe Pennell, who owns the local garage, is going to collect your car first thing in the morning. As for the break-in, the police will look into that. They'll probably want to interview you. And the Fawcetts, who look after the static for your friends will see to the cleaning and repairs. Everything should be back to normal in a couple of days. And as from tomorrow, Mrs Barrett will let you stay with her as long as it's necessary.'

Ben's head came around the corner of the kitchen door, where he had been rattling pots and pans and whistling merrily to himself as he worked. The aroma that accompanied the sound was mouth-wateringly delicious.

'Why can't Judith stay here with us, Dad?' he asked, his forehead creasing into a frown. 'After all, the stat's just up the hill. You can see it from your bedroom window.'

'Yes, well . . . ' Rory looked as if he were indeed pondering the question, then he shook his head. 'I don't think that's a good idea, son. Besides, Mrs Barrett can look after Judith far better than we can.'

Ben thought about his father's words, then pulled a face and shrugged his shoulders. 'Yeah, I suppose you're right. I was just looking forward to . . . ' He broke off, looked surreptitiously at Judith and shrugged again. 'Oh, well. Never mind.'

'You get on with the dinner, laddie, while I show Judith to her room. Take the dog with you and find him a basket. He'll be all right in the old back scullery.'

Because of Judith's sodden state, she had headed immediately for the bath-room on arrival at the vet's cottage. Bertie had attached himself to Ben and was enjoying being made a fuss of by a new friend. Now, feeling refreshed, dry and clean once more, Judith clutched her holdall to her and followed Rory along a narrow passage to a door at the end.

'It hasn't been used for a long while,'

he told her as he pushed the door back, allowing her to pass in front of him. 'But it's clean and I've put fresh sheets on the bed.'

'It's very nice, thank you,' she said as she let her eyes travel over the large double bed and the feminine pink drapes. Not exactly her taste, but in the circumstances she considered herself to be very lucky.

'If you would like to hang some of your things up, I'm sure there's space in the wardrobe.'

He pulled open the wardrobe door and Judith saw him stiffen as his gaze fell upon a collection of feminine clothes that swung gently from their hangers. A muscle in his cheek twitched and he seemed to have difficulty swallowing.

'I'm sorry,' he said, recovering and closing the door again with an abrupt movement. 'They were my late wife's clothes. I forgot they were there. This was our room before . . . '

'Please don't worry about it,' Judith

told him quickly, not really knowing what to say for the best. 'I shan't need to hang anything up.'

'I . . . er . . . I moved out into the spare bedroom when she became really ill. It meant that both of us could sleep without being disturbed, though she didn't sleep much towards the end.'

Judith chewed on her lip and wished he hadn't opened that wardrobe door. It was obviously difficult for him to talk about the past, and the sight of his wife's clothes, hanging there like that, must have given him quite a jolt.

'Anyway,' he continued. 'Mustn't bore you with details.'

'It's all right, really,' she said.

He frowned down at the floor between them. 'I can't imagine how I came to forget . . . I meant to clear her things out, but . . . '

The silence fell heavily between them. Judith found it difficult, because he was a stranger. She knew nothing about him. Had he been a friend, she might have thrown her arms about him

31

and hugged him tightly. But he wasn't a friend and she doubted that he would appreciate a hug from her anyway. He didn't seem the kind of man who allowed people to get close. Unlike his son.

On cue, Ben shouted from the kitchen that dinner was ready. Judith gave the boy a mental hug for coming to her rescue so opportunely, and not for the first time that evening.

4

'I don't know why he didn't just bring you back here in the first place!' Judith was sitting in Mrs Barrett's warm kitchen, having been transported there by Rory on his way to see an injured cow on the other side of the valley. He had hardly spoken to her during the short journey and she gave up trying to make small talk after the first five minutes.

'Well, it would have suited me fine,' Judith told the farmer's wife with a grimace. 'I got the impression that an unexpected visitor was the last thing he wanted to contend with last night. And this morning — well, he couldn't wait to get rid of me.'

'Ach, lassie, don't judge the poor man too harshly,' Mrs Barrett said, and refilled Judith's cup with surprisingly good coffee. 'It's the boy's fault, in a way, that he's so prickly and on his guard.'

'Ben? But he's such a friendly soul . . . '

'Aye, he is, that, but ye see, for the past two or three years, Ben's been trying to get his father matched up with one female or another — and Heaven knows, the pair of them could do with the influence of a good woman in their lives, but Rory will have none of it.'

'Oh, I see — well, I think I do.'

Irritation was giving way to confusion in Judith's head. The vet's house had certainly seemed a bit sparse and unloved. It had been tidy enough, and basically clean, but there was no feminine touches to speak of, apart from the room she had slept in. She had noticed a photograph in a silver frame of a much younger Rory, arm in arm with a pretty, smiling girl holding a small child in her arms, which she assumed was Ben. They looked happy.

Mrs Barrett shook her head sadly and continued to gossip. 'They have many an argument over it. You see, m'dear, Rory is dead set against any woman stepping into the shoes of his poor dead wife, though plenty of them around here have tried and failed miserably. He's not a man who is easily moved is Rory Telford. Pig-headed, ye might say, when it comes to matters of the heart particularly.'

Judith sighed. 'In that case, I suppose I should be grateful that he took the trouble to help me in the first place, not to mention sorting everything out regarding my car and the static caravan.'

'Oh, don't get me wrong, girl,' Mrs Barrett said. 'He has a heart of gold, that one. He just doesn't wear it on his sleeve any more, not like he used to.'

Judith put her cup down and eyed the strawberry jam tarts on the table in front of her, but decided against having another one.

'It must have been very traumatic,' she said, 'losing his wife at such a young age. I was young when I lost my parents, but it's not quite the same, is it?'

'No, dear, it's not.'

Mrs Barrett shook her head and went to take out a steak and kidney pie from the huge Age cooker that was throwing out enough heat to melt iron.

'They lost a child, you know. A lovely little girl. You probably saw a photo of them with her . . . '

'Oh, I thought it was Ben, but now you come to mention it, it did look more like a girl.'

'Aye. Katie, they called her. She was killed when she was only a toddler. The gate had been left open and she wandered out on to the road. Laura blamed Rory at the time. Of course, they never got over it. Ben came along a few months later, but by the time he started school Laura had been diagnosed with cancer. Ben was a lovely child, but somehow Laura never seemed very close to the poor wee mite.'

'It must have been hard for both of them.'

'Especially Rory. He spent all his time looking after Laura while trying to be both mother and father to Ben. Och, I shouldn't be telling you all this. It's boring old stuff. My husband says I gossip too much, and he's probably right. Now, then, Judith, tell me your story. Something's put the sadness into those pretty eyes of yours . . . '

★ ★ ★

It was three days before Judith was able to move into the static caravan, and she was more than glad to have her own company at last. Kind-hearted though Mrs Barrett was, she tended to talk non-stop until Judith's head resounded with the sound of the constant chatter.

Maggie and George had been reassured that all was being taken care of. Thankfully, there had been no real damage apart from the broken door and window. Once the place had been cleaned up and the necessary repairs effected, it was impossible to tell that

37

the break-in had ever occurred.

Maggie, of course, sounded a little frantic on the other end of the telephone. She was worried about Judith being on her own, and had to be reminded that Bertie could get more than a little protective if the wrong people came to call.

'Oh, well, it's up to you, of course, but I would feel nervous after what's happened. Can't you get a room at the local inn or something, where there are people?'

'Maggie, the reason I'm here in the first place is to get away from people. Look, I'll be fine. Anyway, it's not so isolated as all that. I can look down the valley and see the vet's house.'

'Oh, Dr Telford's place? Yes, I forgot to tell you about him.'

'I've already met him,' she said, carefully omitting to tell her friend the bit about staying the night. Maggie would be horrified at the thought. 'And the local farmer's wife has filled me in on all the details.'

'About the woman he's got in the village, do you mean?'

Judith blinked in surprise at Maggie's revelation.

'That's strange! I rather got the impression that he's a bit of a woman-hater since his wife died.'

'Ha! I'm sure that's what he likes people to think, but George and I have seen him with her. We've seen Rory Telford frequently visit a certain woman who lives in the cottage opposite the tavern — it does good food, by the way. I'm not talking here about veterinary visits either. Years older than him, too. And, it was going on long before his wife died.'

'Yes, well . . . '

Judith hesitated, not sure what she was expected to say. She was loath to believe what she had just heard. It was unlike Maggie to spread malicious gossip, but she didn't usually get things wrong.

'I'm just telling you,' Maggie continued, 'because that man has apparently broken more hearts than Rudolph Valentino and I wouldn't want you to get involved with anyone like that.'

'Who's Rudolph Valentino when he's at home?' Judith grinned; she always liked to tease her friend, who was an easy prey.

'Oh, I keep forgetting how young you are!' Maggie's sigh of exasperation hissed in her ear. 'Look, Judith, don't be taken in by those good looks and the lost air of his. You're very vulnerable at the moment and love on the rebound has been known to destroy lives.'

'I don't think you have any need to worry, Maggie,' she said quickly, before a full lecture got under way. 'I don't even like the man.'

'In that case, there's no problem. Now, if you're sure you're all right, enjoy our *Rose Cottage* and treat it as if it's your own.'

'Thanks, Maggie, I will. Now, I must go and see what's upsetting Bertie. He's barking his head off.'

'I can hear him. Take care, love!'

'Don't I always?'

Bertie was putting on his best neurotic act for the benefit of someone or other who had managed to get through the gate without being detected. The dog had the person pinned to a broad-trunked oak tree half way down the garden.

'Down, Bertie!' she screamed as she ran forward, always on the alert in case her beloved companion savaged anyone, for he was not the most tolerant of dogs.

Judith could see the sharp, canine teeth, bared and gnashing, and she imagined she could even smell the fear of Bertie's unfortunate victim. She grabbed for the dog's collar and pulled him back, and the pungent odour got worse.

'Gawd, I thought I wus a gonner there, missus! You should keep that thing on a chain.'

'What are you doing here?' she demanded, recognising the tramp she had encountered the night of the storm.

'This is private property and . . . '

'I come to apologise,' the tramp said and before she could think of another thing to say, he thrust a bunch of flowers at her, one eye fixed warily on Bertie.

'Apologise?'

'Aye, though it weren't me wot broke the window of that there caravan, nor the door neither. I found it that way, honest I did, missus.'

The old tramp was still shoving the flowers at her. So she felt obliged to take them, surprised to find that they weren't flowers from anyone's garden, but were wild flowers that grew on the hillsides.

Judith frowned at him. 'If you weren't responsible for the damage, why do you feel the need to apologise?'

He sniffed and looked uneasy, then wiped his coat sleeve across his face. ''Cos I spent a coupl' a nights in there, and I knows I shouldn't, but me shed was blown down an' it was bitter enough to freeze the . . . well, anyways

. . . that's how it was.'

Bertie had calmed down at last and was busily sniffing around the tramp's ankles where his ragged trousers were tied with string to keep out the draughts. Judith remembered how Ben Telford had told her that Fred was harmless and this unexpected gesture on his part surely bore out the boy's judgment.

'I've just made a pot of tea,' she said uncertainly and saw the old fellow's eyes light up. 'Would you like some?'

'I don't mind if I do, missus.' He went and sat on an old timber bench while she fetched him a mug of steaming tea and a ham sandwich. 'That's grand of ye. The vet's lad said you was a lady. Cheers, missus!'

Fifteen minutes later, Fred set off happily, back to his shed, which he claimed to have fixed. Before he left, Judith gave him the roast chicken she had planned for supper, plus a few other items, including a thick blanket that she had spare.

'Yer a right queen, missus,' he said, his watery eyes flashing like beacons of gratitude. 'When I see young Ben again I'll tell him he was right about you. Class, he said you was an' class is wot you are.'

5

Having given away her supper, Judith decided to treat herself to a meal out and remembered what Maggie had said about the tavern in the village. It was already too late to book, so she would just have to take a chance on it not being full.

The name of the restaurant and a little map on how to find it was pinned on Maggie's notice board hanging on the wall in the kitchen area. Toby's Tavern was a good ten minutes drive away, but when she saw how cosy it was with its inglenook, its open fires and touches of warming red everywhere, she was glad that she had come.

They served old-fashioned English fayre and she felt a twinge of guilt at choosing rich minced beef and crispy dumplings with apple crumble and cream for dessert. Still, she had lost a lot of weight while going through the rigours of divorce, so she could afford to gain a few pounds now. And this was food therapy of the best kind she was offering herself this evening.

It was late and inky black outside by the time she was sipping a glass of steaming Irish coffee to finish off the delicious meal. The tavern was almost empty, though it had been full and buzzing with jovial conversation when she arrived.

The scrape of a chair in a booth somewhere at the far end of the room, followed by a deep-throated chuckle and a subdued conversation, attracted her attention. There was something familiar about the man's voice. As the couple approached, heading for the door, Judith lifted her head and found her eyes meeting those of Rory Telford.

He looked a trifle startled to see her. Judith toyed with pretending she had not seen him, remembering what Maggie had told her, but then she thought better of it and smiled. Well, if he had his guilty secrets it was none of her business. Let him get on with it.

'Good evening!' The vet had recovered his apparent embarrassment, and was approaching her table after a few whispered words in his companion's ear. 'Nice to see you taking advantage of the local hostelry.'

'My friends recommended it,' Judith told him, smiling at the woman who stood patiently at his elbow. 'And they were right. The food is excellent, though I don't think I can afford to eat here too often. Too many calories.'

The woman laughed and nodded. She had a plain face that became pretty when she laughed and it was a pleasant sound.

'I know what you mean,' she told Judith, patting her slightly overweight midriff. 'And once you pass fifty it gets too easy to put weight on and almost impossible to lose it.'

An irritable frown creased Rory Telford's forehead and he brushed a hand across it as if to wipe it away.

'I'm sorry, I'm forgetting my manners. This is Sarah, a good friend of mine. Sarah, this is Judith, who has come to stay in the static caravan on the hill behind my house.'

'Ah! I thought I hadn't seen you before. It's such a small world around here, we all tend to know one another — to a certain degree.'

She had hesitated before the last few words as though they were supposed to be meaningful. A second later Rory's hand was cupping his companion's elbow and he seemed to be urging her back towards the door.

'I haven't had a chance to thank you properly, yet,' Judith said to him, and saw a slight twitch of a facial muscle. 'It was so good of you to help me out.'

'It was the least I could do,' he said almost brusquely. 'I take it everything is OK now?'

'Everything's fine, thank you.'

'Well, goodnight.'

The woman called Sarah smiled curiously, her eyes travelling from Rory to Judith, then back again. Judith bade them both goodnight and then they were gone and she felt strangely alone.

She peered out of the window and was in time to see the vet and his somewhat older companion cross the gravel road, heads bent together in an intimately muttered conversation. There was a flash of amber light as a door opened and they disappeared into the large house opposite. A fraction of a second passed before the windows were illuminated with the same warm glow.

Judith felt a dullness creep through her and wondered how long it would take before the lights went out, and if Rory Telford would still be there when they did.

For some odd reason, she didn't feel that she wanted to stay long enough to find out.

6

As the days slid by into weeks and the weather improved, Judith began to feel more settled. There was always something to do around the garden, and the van was constantly full of sweet-smelling roses.

She lived with the perfume all around her and as the temperature rose, so did the fragrance. It was heady and romantic and it reminded her too acutely of what was missing from her life.

Judith's most constant visitor was old Fred, the tramp. She imagined that Maggie would have turned him away, but Judith didn't have the heart. Besides, he was helpful in the garden and seemed to know, better than her, how to care for Maggie's precious plants.

'This plant here needs a lot of water,

see,' he would say. 'And that there Hosta doesn't like too much sun.'

When it was possible to eat outside, Judith took to inviting Fred to join her. Eating inside was not an option, since the old fellow stank to high heaven most of the time. She always made sure that she was sitting upwind of him, and at a strategic distance.

She even came to look forward to his visits. And Bertie had taken to lying docilely at the tramp's feet, gazing up at him with adoring eyes, not in the least put out by the aromas that lingered in the air.

Judith had hoped for a visit from at least one of the Telfords, but that was not to be, it seemed. Ben had visited a couple of times, then stopped. Weeks had passed and not a sign of either father or son. Why she should find this disappointing she could not work out. After all, she had come here to get away from people. Why should she suddenly be craving company?

'There you are, Fred,' she said as she

handed the tramp a plate of food, which he took humbly now, without grabbing it as if he were starving.

'Ye're a right star!' he exclaimed, examining every morsel with a beady eye. 'I likes a nice lamb chop and here you are giving me three of 'em, I ask ye! Ye're too good to me, missus.'

'Not at all, Fred. It's a fair exchange.' Judith beamed at him as he ate hungrily. 'After all, you do plenty for me. It's only fair that I should feed you in exchange.'

'Aye, lass. It's better than giving me money. With money I just goes and spends it on booze and that doesn't do anybody any good, so thank ye kindly.'

She watched as he took the largest of the lamb chops in his fingers and sucked off the tender meat, his eyes rolling with gratification. Then he looked about him, as he always did, calling for Bertie to come and share the feast.

'Where is he?' he asked, when the dog didn't appear at the gallop.

7

Judith stood up and looked about her. Now that Fred had mentioned it, Bertie had been keeping a very low profile all day. In fact, he had been a little quiet all week. Too quiet for a dog that was used to making a grand fuss at the least thing. But then he was fifteen, and in doggy language that was quite elderly. He had to start slowing down sometime.

'I don't know where he's got to, Fred,' she said, trying not to feel panicky. 'Maybe it's too hot for him out here.'

She got up and went into the van and there, sure enough, was her best pal, lying at the foot of her bed, looking slightly sheepish, a big smile on his face, pink tongue lolling as he panted a greeting, his big ears working like radar antennae.

'There you are, sweetheart!' she cried

out in relief, but noticed that the dog did not rise to come to her as he usually did. 'Yes, it's too darned hot today, isn't it, Bertie?'

She bent to stroke his silky head and he licked her hand. Checking that he had enough water and food close to hand, she returned to her supper guest with the news that all was well.

'He's an old warrior,' Fred said, 'just like me.'

'You're right there, Fred,' Judith agreed, lifting a hand to shade her eyes as she saw a moving figure on the hill coming towards them.

'It's the vet's boy,' Fred informed her, squinting into the lowering sun with narrowed eyes that missed nothing.

Judith's heart leapt and she had to ask herself why. She certainly wasn't hankering after a seventeen-year-old schoolboy, and his father was far too preoccupied with his own affairs to be more than civil at a distance.

'Hi!' Ben raised his arm in salute as he drew closer.

'Hello, Ben!' Judith called back, aware of Fred picking up his belongings and moving away. 'No, Fred, you don't have to go.'

'Oh, I've eaten my fill, missus, and I thanks ye, but I don't want to appear to be a nuisance, now, do I?'

'You're not a nuisance, Fred. You're a friend.'

The tramp's eyes misted over. He licked his lips and touched a finger to his forelock, a pathetic strand of grey hair that fell from a balding pate.

'That'll be a first,' he said, nodding vigorously. 'But I'll be off anyhows. The boy won't be wantin' to talk to ye in front of me, that he won't.'

'All right, Fred. Have it your way.'

'I usually does, missus,' Fred muttered as he loped off with a semi-trotting gait, leaving a whiff of himself dwindling in the evening air.

Judith watched him go, then turned her attention on her visitor. Ben looked vaguely uncomfortable, she thought, as he approached her slowly.

'Hello, Ben,' she said. 'You haven't been around much lately.'

'Yes, I know, I'm sorry.' He stood before her, his hands stuffed into his trouser pockets.

'You don't have to apologise. I'm sure you have better things to do than visit me.' She gave him a warm smile when she saw him frown. 'Like some home-made lemonade?'

He shook his head. 'Thanks, but I've just had a beer.' He saw her quick look and his mouth tweaked into a smile. 'It's all right. I'm eighteen now . . . well, as of today.'

'Oh, Ben! Had I known I'd have sent you a card or baked a cake or something.'

He shrugged and shifted the patch of gritty soil at his feet. There was something on his mind that he seemed to be having difficulty saying. Judith looked at him and waited patiently.

'I'm starting at university next week,' he said eventually.

'That's wonderful. Are you still

planning on becoming a chef?'

'Yes, but Dad wants me to have a full education behind me before I go down that road . . . ' He glanced up at her, half-smiling, half-frowning. 'It's all right . . . I'm cool with that. It's just . . . '

'What's the problem, Ben? I can see that something is bothering you.'

She heard his intake of breath, saw his chest rise and fall slowly as he chewed over what was going on in his head.

'Look, please don't tell Dad that I was here, will you.' Ben looked about him furtively as if expecting his father to pop out from behind the nearest tree. 'He made me promise I would stay away and not bother you, but . . . '

Judith was appalled. 'Why on earth would he do that? Does he think I'm some kind of bad influence or something?'

'No! Nothing like that.' Ben's face flushed scarlet. 'It's just that . . . oh, hell! Sorry!'

'I think you'd better tell me what this

is all about, Ben, because if you don't I'll go right down there and demand a response from your father.'

'No, don't do that, Judith.'

'Then tell me.'

Ben's shoulders worked up and down, then he blurted it out. 'The thing is, my dad's going to be on his own now that I'm going to uni. I thought that you and he might . . . well, get together, you know.'

'Ben! Are you playing Cupid or Devil's Advocate?'

'Devil's Advocate?'

'Well, what about . . . ' Judith hesitated, then decided it might be indiscreet to mention that woman, Sarah, to Ben. Perhaps his father was keeping the relationship a secret from him too. 'Never mind, Ben.'

'Don't you like my father?'

Judith's eyebrows lifted, then descended into an uncertain frown.

'I rather thought that he didn't like me too much,' she said.

'He puts on an act so people won't

get the wrong idea. I keep telling him that he should get out more and socialise, but . . . '

'Perhaps he feels he's being unfaithful to your mother, Ben. It's not easy getting over the loss of a loved one.'

'I know that, but it's been years since Mum died and she was pretty ill for years before that. Anyway, I just thought I'd tell you that — well, he's great really, and I'm sure he does like you, honest.'

'I'll take your word for it,' Judith said with a light laugh. 'But Ben, it doesn't do any good trying to play matchmaker. There has to be a certain magic between two people before they can even start to think of romance.'

Ben nodded solemnly and Judith half expected a remark about romance being an old-fashioned word, the meaning of which no longer existed today. She pretty much believed, herself, that romance was dead. At least as far as she was concerned, and she certainly wasn't going to get involved with any man just for the sake of it.

It would take more than Rory Telford's good looks to tempt her, even if his son thought it was a good idea to push them together.

'Well, see you around,' Ben said. 'Sorry I bothered you.'

The boy started to walk away. It was the first time Judith had seen him looking sulky.

'I hope everything works out for you at university,' she called out after him and he turned back, arms akimbo, palms facing her.

'Actually,' he said with a determined air. 'I do know about that magic that happens between two people. It happened to me ages ago, but Dad just gets irritable when I try to talk to him about it. He doesn't believe in magic any more.'

'Oh, I see.'

Well, Judith thought, they did have something in common after all.

'There's this girl, Penny,' Ben continued. 'I met her when I was fifteen and we've been together ever since. Dad thinks I'm too young to settle down, but I can't imagine life without her, you know?'

Oh, yes. Judith knew all about that feeling. Hadn't she experienced it with Tim? She thought their love would last forever. But it hadn't and now she was divorced and trying to persuade herself that life was far better without relationships.

'It's always like that, Ben. And then something happens and you get hurt. Later, when you meet someone else, you start all over again.'

'I knew you'd say that,' Ben came back and stood close so that his voice wouldn't carry half way down the valley to any ears that might be hungry for scandal. 'Look, Judith, I'll level with you. I kind of hoped you and Dad would get together so he wouldn't bother about me and my life so much.'

'Oh, so you thought I'd take him off your back, eh?' Judith smiled broadly, understanding exactly where this young man was coming from.

'Something like that, but actually, if you ever did . . . you know . . . get together, that would be fine with me. I really like you, Judith.'

'Unfortunately, it's your father who has to like me before a relationship of any kind can develop. Up to now, I get the feeling that he just thinks of me as an inconvenience.'

'Yes, I know,' Ben shuffled his feet. 'He can be pig-headed, but I know he likes you. He just won't admit it.'

'I think that's just a bit of wishful thinking on your part, Ben. However, I am flattered.'

'It's not just wishful thinking. I've seen him standing in his window gazing up here, and when your name's mentioned he goes all quiet, or changes the subject. And he tells me I'm immature. I ask you.'

Judith laughed, then found a way to steer the conversation away from the subject of the ill-mannered vet. A few minutes later she sent Ben off, having extracted a promise that he would bring his girlfriend to meet her one day.

She went back to the caravan and found Bertie lying in a darkened corner, his head on his paws, snoring gently. It was odd that he had not come to greet Ben, who had made such a fuss of him. Perhaps her old pal was sickening for something after all.

'Oh, dear, Bertie,' she sighed and ran a hand down his thick white coat. 'Please don't be ill.' If he wasn't back to normal in the morning she would have to take him to Dr Telford, and the stupid man might get the wrong idea and . . .

Her words tailed off and she heaved another sigh. 'Now who's being stupid,' she said to herself. 'This is not about you.'

It wouldn't do any harm to have Rory Telford give Bertie the once over. Maybe he'd picked up a tic or something. You couldn't take chances with any animal's health and Bertie was so very precious to her it would be worth the humiliation of a visit.

As if he understood, the dog gave a whine and nuzzled her hand, then got up with difficulty and waddled drunkenly to the door, looking at her plaintively over his shoulder. It was time for him to do what dogs have to do before he bedded down for the night and Bertie was a very clean, proud animal.

8

The storm that came in the night took Judith by surprise. There had been no warning signs, though the days leading up to it were unbearably hot and humid. This, she supposed, heralded the end of summer and the beginning of autumn.

She was well accustomed to the kind of bad weather that often swept over the Lake District, but this storm was the most violent she had experienced so far.

Once again, it took out the power, but this time she was prepared and knew where to put her hands on candles and matches, Bertie had not gone berserk, as the thunder crackled and banged about above their heads and that worried her even more.

'Bertie? Are you all right, boy?'

She finished lighting candles, the light from them filling the van with a pale, flickering glow. Turning, she saw that the dog was lying in his basket, mournful eyes turned in her direction. He gave a small whimper, then tucked his nose beneath his tail.

That decided it. Tomorrow, come hell or high water, she would take him down the hill to get Rory Telford's professional opinion. And she would just have to put up with the vet's brusque attitude and the fact that he seemed to want to distance himself from her, for reasons best known to himself.

The thunder continued, sounding so much louder and more frightening in the van that it would in a more substantial building. For a while, Judith thought about old Fred and hoped that he was cosy and dry in his shack. She would make a point of checking on him tomorrow.

Despite her expectations to the contrary, she did finally drift off to sleep, though a particularly loud clap of thunder jolted her back to consciousness. She lay with a palpitating heart, blinking into the darkness.

There was still no electricity and her luminous bedside clock told her, amazingly, that it was seven-thirty. Outside, there was that eerie light that storms often created.

She could see purplish black clouds boiling above, dancing tree silhouettes against luminous patches of struggling green dawn. The van rocked ominously as the wind rushed at it, shaking it almost from its moorings like an old tin can.

Good Lord, she whispered to herself as she once more lit candles and struggled to get dressed. This was no ordinary storm. Poor Fred would be lucky if his shack stood up to the gale force wind being so strong. Outside, the light was turning from black to opalescent grey and she stifled a gasp of horror as she saw what had caused the noise.

A large conifer had come down. If that wasn't bad enough in itself, it had come down right across Judith's car, crushing the roof and the bonnet, and was now resting like a gigantic seesaw, its spiky top on the ground, its broad base and shallow roots in the air pouring with muddy water.

Judith swallowed hard and bit down on her lip. For an instant all her senses seemed to shut down. Her brain could no longer function. She had to do something, but what?

'Come on, Judith.' She spoke aloud to give herself courage, 'Priorities first. The car's replaceable.'

Scrabbling about behind the door, she came up with an ample yellow waterproof that must have belonged to George, because it came down to her ankles. Still, in this kind of weather she was going to need all the protection she could get.

'Bertie?' She looked back into the dimness of the van and decided that her poor dog was far too scared to want to attempt his usual morning sortie. 'Stay here, OK? I'll be back, sweetheart.'

The first thing that happened when

she stepped out of the van was that her shoes filled with water. She could feel the silty slush of it squishing between her toes as she walked, but she couldn't afford to waste time looking for wellingtons. Having wet feet was the least of her worries.

Slowly, and with her heart in her mouth, Judith made her way down the hillside in the direction of Fred's shack. Fortunately, the flashlight worked a treat since she had replaced the worn out old batteries and she swung it from side to side as she strode out, looking a lot braver, she was sure, than she felt.

Picking her way with care, she descended to the narrow track leading to the tramp's humble abode. The ground was running with ankle-deep water and the sodden mud sucked at her feet with every step she took. It was difficult to see because of the way the rain bleached this way and that and she had to dodge the whipping of the lower tree branches.

She seemed to be walking for a long

time and there was still no recognisable sign to fix her eyes on. Surely, she would have come across the shack before now, she reasoned. Swinging the flashlight around in a complete arc now, she saw the total devastation that had been wrought by the ongoing storm.

Trees were down everywhere. A few yards away a telegraph pole was lying at an angle and snapped wires were flying about like bulldog thongs. As she watched, in awe, another wire snapped and sent a shower of sparks into the turbulent skies above.

Then she heard a familiar noise. A bark, faint, a little weak, but unmistakably Bertie. The dog must have followed her. She made her way towards the sound, calling his name, willing her eyes to see far beyond her capabilities.

And there, suddenly, in front of her, was the bobbing rear end of Bertie, white plumed tail wagging furiously. He was digging among a pile of shattered wood, grunting, barking and whining all at the same time. She knew instantly that the pile of wood was the remains of Fred's shack and, judging by Bertie's behaviour, Fred was buried underneath it somewhere.

Judith laid the flashlight on the ground and wedged it secure with a couple of heavy stones.

'Fred!' she cried out, desperately, joining the dog and pulling at the timbers with her bare hands. 'Fred, can you hear me?'

Even if he responded, Judith would not have been able to hear it above the still raging storm. However, she was sure he must be in there, and her faith in the old dog was soon rewarded. Bertie had his teeth in a piece of dark material and he was pulling for all he was worth. Then she saw a hand emerge from the debris that had once been Fred's home, which he had regarded as a palace.

9

On her hands and knees now, ignoring the splintered wood and the rusty nails and shattered glass, Judith continued to tear at the pile of rubble. It seemed to take forever to get to him, but at last he was free, and still breathing, though he was covered in blood.

'Is that you, missus?' he moaned weakly, and she cried out in relief at the sound of his voice.

'It's me, Fred,' she said, breathless and choking as the wind battered her. 'How badly are you hurt?'

'I'll do,' he muttered as he attempted to stand, though his legs buckled beneath his weight. ''Twas that ugly dog of yours wot saved me.'

'He's not ugly,' Judith said, supporting him as best she could and trying to move forward, one step at a time. 'He's the most beautiful dog in the world and don't you say otherwise, Fred.'

'Ay, lass, ye're right an' all, bless him.'

All the way back to the van, Bertie walked as close to Judith as she could get, pressing himself against her leg. It was difficult making progress like that, Bertie on one side of her, Fred on the other, and the storm all around. But they made it.

Once inside the van, even in candle-light Judith could see that Fred was in a pretty bad way. She suspected a sprained ankle and a dislocated shoulder, but he was also having difficulty breathing and cried out involuntarily when he moved or coughed. And there was a telltale blueness about his lips that she didn't like at all.

'Fred, I think maybe you've cracked a rib or two. I'm going to call for an ambulance.'

'I'm all right, lass. I've had worse in my lifetime.'

'Even so . . . ' She was frowning at her cell phone in disbelief. Nothing she did would bring it to life. It was as dead as the proverbial dodo.

Great, she thought. No car, no phone, the granddaddy of all storms and I've got a sick old man on my hands.

'Fred, I . . . ' She turned back to the tramp and stared in horror as she saw him clutch at his chest and fall back on to her bed with a gasp. 'Fred?'

'I'm sorry, missus . . . fer the trouble I's caused ye . . . ' He lay staring at the ceiling, struggling to breath, a dribble of saliva rolling down his chin, his eyes glazed. 'Not an ugly dog, Bertie. Proud to be his pal . . . an' yours too, missus . . . '

'Oh, Fred, please don't die!' Judith whispered fearfully as she saw him slowly lose consciousness.

★   ★   ★

She refused to panic. This was something she had to deal with logically and sensibly. Acting the frantically neurotic female would help no-one. Judith tucked a blanket around Fred and ran shaking fingers through her hair.

She looked down at Bertie, who was wet and muddy and quivering from head to foot, his chin resting on the edge of the bed as he watched over the comatose figure.

'I've got to get help for Fred,' she said aloud as she quickly towelled the dog dry and turned up the thermostat of the Calor gas heating system. At least she could leave them warm and dry while she went in search of help.

* * *

There was only one place she could reach on foot, and so Judith headed there without pause for thought. Rory Telford was a vet and the next best thing to a doctor. He would know what to do. She just prayed that they could get help to Fred before it was too late.

Slipping and slithering all the way, she half-walked, half-ran in the direction of Rory's cottage. Twice she ended up on her behind, and once on her hands and knees as she struggled to keep her footing on the rough, water-logged ground. She could have stuck to the track, but that was running like a raging river and would have taken twice as long that way.

'Dr Telford!' Judith cried out as loudly as she could as she came within shouting distance of the cottage. 'Dr Telford! Rory!'

Oh, please let him be there, she prayed, for the place was still in darkness, although she knew him to be an early riser. Of course, the electricity wires were probably down throughout the valley.

She put her expectation on power failure and not absence and threw herself at the door of the cottage, pounding it with her fists between thunderous blasts from above. After a while, when her hands hurt from beating the wood, all to no avail, Judith felt an icy shiver creep up her spine. It was painfully clear that no one was at home.

There was no time to rest. She struck out once more in the direction of the village, grateful that it was finally daylight and she could at least see where she was going, despite the wind-lashed rain hitting her full in the face.

She must have covered half the distance and was ready to drop when a pair of headlights turned the bend in the road ahead. The lights belonged to a large Land-Rover, its windscreen wipers working overtime, its huge tyres throwing up black, watery mud in every direction.

Judith placed herself in the middle of the road, arms and legs stretched out, waving, shouting at the driver. The vehicle stopped with only inches to spare and she staggered to the side window that had been lowered.

'Please, you've got to help me . . . ' She broke off as she recognised the driver.

'Judith? What on earth?' She stared in surprised at Rory Telford's equally astonished face and there was a bleep of silence between them before he pushed open the passenger door and ordered her to get in.

'Everything's in chaos,' she told him, trying to mop her face with a sodden square of handkerchief, aware for the first time of water running in cold rivulets down her neck. 'Fred's shack got hit by the storm and collapsed on top of him. He's badly hurt. My car has a fir tree sitting on it, there's no electricity, my phone isn't working and . . . and . . . oh, God, I'm so glad to see you, Rory!'

'Take it easy,' Rory flashed her a worried look, then concentrated on the driving, which was about as much as anybody could do in the circumstances. 'Calm down, woman.'

'I am calm, blast you!' she yelled at him and saw his eyebrows flick up and down. 'OK, OK, so I'm frantic, but I'm going to calm down now, see?'

She held out her hands before her and gave a small, hysterical laugh as she saw how much they were shaking.

'Look in the side compartment,' he ordered. 'There's a bottle of whisky in there. Take a couple of large swigs.'

'Thank you,' she said meekly, then, when the medicinal alcohol had done its trick she turned curious eyes on her rescuer. 'I went to your cottage, but you weren't there.'

She thought she saw him flinch, but he kept his eyes on the road ahead.

'I spent the night at Sarah's,' he said as if it were something he did often. 'My jeep got waterlogged and she loaned me this beauty so I could get home. Lucky thing, really. This is the only vehicle for miles around that's capable of getting to your van in this weather.'

'Yes,' she said, her thoughts weighing heaving inside her. 'Yes, very lucky.'

10

It took a few minutes for Rory to call in at his cottage and collect some medical supplies, then they were on their way again. By the time they arrived at the static van, Judith had recovered some of her strength and her nerves had settled down to a minor rather a major jangle.

Fred recovered consciousness briefly as Rory examined him and confirmed Judith's fears. He patched the old tramp up as best he could, but if anything was going to save Fred's life it would be the speed with which he could get specialist cardiac care.

'Right, Fred,' Rory said with gentle authority. 'We're going to get you to hospital. It's going to be a rough ride, I'm afraid, but we're all you've got right now because of this blessed storm.'

'Don't worry about me, none,' Fred whispered. 'I'll be all right, but I don't like the look of that there dog, see.'

Judith and Rory turned to look at Bertie. The dog was braced up against the corner of a cupboard unit, sitting at a peculiar angle, his head to one side, smiling absurdly, his pink tongue lolling.

'What's wrong, boy?' Judith was rooted to the spot as she watched her Bertie struggle to his three feet and try to reach her on legs that didn't seem to know which direction to take.

'Oh, Bertie!' She sank down to her knees in front of him and he tried to lick her face, but got it all wrong and just sank down and looked at her with that imbecile canine grin. She could almost hear him saying, '*Oh, Mum, look what's happened to me now!*'

She glanced up at Rory, but he was too busy lifting Fred and staggering out in the storm with him.

'Come on, Judith,' he shouted over his shoulder. 'You can't stay here now. This whole hillside looks in danger of sliding.'

'Oh, but . . . ' She looked back at Bertie, her heart aching for him.

'We don't have time to argue,' was the response and she knew what he was implying. If they delayed much longer, Fred could die.

Then he heard a weak voice coming from the blanketed figure in Rory's arms.

'That dog saved my life, mister. Don't you leave him behind. You gotta help him.'

'I have no intention of leaving him behind,' Rory said, casting a glance over his shoulder as he heaved his patient into the back seat of the Land Rover. 'Come on, Judith. What are you waiting for? Bring the dog, will you?'

She bent and scooped Bertie up in her arms like a baby. He was damp and dirty and reeked of wet dog, but she didn't care, as long as she didn't have to leave him. She would have walked into the village with him in her arms if necessary.

Fred was strapped into the back passenger seat, the extent of his injuries making him groan sporadically. Rory turned to Judith.

'Give Bertie to me,' he said. 'You get in.'

Once she was safely installed, Rory handed her the dog and she cuddled him to her as they started off in the direction of the village. The broad tyres of the Land Rover had difficulty finding purchase on the washed out road, but Rory was doing a piece of impressive driving, for which she was more than thankful.

★   ★   ★

When he pulled in, blasting his horn, in front of the house opposite the tavern, Judith was puzzled. She remembered this house. It was the one she had seen Rory enter with that woman, Sarah.

'What are you doing?' she demanded as he leaned on the horn yet again.

'Get out,' he said.

'What!'

'Judith, do as I say, for goodness

sake. Get out so I can take Fred on to the hospital.'

'But . . . ' She could see the door of the house opening, see Sarah standing there, squinting out curiously. 'I don't understand.'

Rory was out of the vehicle and pulling open her door. He hauled Bertie out of her arms and ran up the short garden path with him, Judith following at the double, her heart racing faster than her legs.

'Sarah,' she heard him say to his friend. 'Do your best here, will you. I have to get old Fred to hospital. It's an emergency both ways.'

He disappeared inside, then emerged seconds later, minus Bertie. Without a further word to either woman he jumped back into the Land Rover and drove off at a speed just short of reckless, but at least the storm appeared to be finally blowing itself out.

'Oh, dear,' the woman said, casting a sympathetic eye over Judith, who was standing on her doorstep, shivering with cold and shock. 'You are in a dreadful state, poor thing. Do come in. I've just lit the fire.'

'Where's Bertie?' Judith asked through chattering teeth as she stepped inside and felt the warmth of the place wrap itself around her. 'Please don't bother about me. My dog is sick.'

'Come through to the back,' the woman told her. 'I'm Sarah, by the way. Rory and I go back a long way.'

'Yes, we met one evening in the tavern.' Judith frowned at Sarah's grey head as she followed her.

'That's right. I remember now. Aren't you living in that static caravan up on the hill?'

'That's right, but I'm beginning to wonder if I should ever have come. We were almost washed away by the storm . . . '

The room they entered was brightly lit by neon tubes and Judith blinked at them in astonishment.

'I have an emergency generator,' Sarah explained. 'I had it installed years ago and never thought to take it out when I retired.'

Judith looked about her and saw that the room was a fully-equipped surgery and Bertie was lying dolefully on his side on an examining table.

He lifted his head and whimpered at her as she approached. She took one of his paws in her hands.

'I don't know what to do for you, sweetheart,' she crooned in his ear, her throat suddenly restricted by suppressed emotion.

'Poor old boy,' Sarah said, pulling on a white coat and approaching the table with a stethoscope in her ears. 'He's in a bad way, I'm afraid.'

'You . . . you're a vet?' Judith asked.

'Yes. Rory was my student, then my partner for a while, until I decided to call it a day. I still help out when I'm needed. There, there, boy, I'm not going to hurt you.'

Bertie had found enough strength to bare his teeth and a low growl rumbled in his throat.

'He's not good with strangers,' Judith told Sarah quickly. 'Is it a stroke? He's been off colour for a few days and then, tonight . . . well, he was quite a little hero, even though he's terrified of storms.'

'Hmm.' Sarah finished her examination and pocketed her stethoscope. 'Frankly, I think he would have had the stroke anyway. I'm afraid the news isn't good, Judith.'

Judith's teeth crunched down on her lip and she felt her eyes prickle with tears. 'He's fifteen. I never expected him to last that long, but it's still hard to think of him going.'

The woman's hand gripped her shoulder and Judith sucked in a gasp of air to stop making a fool of herself.

'He must have been a beautiful dog once,' Sarah said and Judith nodded blindly. 'I can tell he's had a good life, but I have to be honest with you — it's a massive stroke and I doubt he'll ever recover. His heart's far too weak. I think it's time for him to be at peace.'

Judith nodded. She couldn't speak. It wasn't totally unexpected. Bertie had been living on borrowed time for a while now. She had been prepared for this, but it didn't stop it hurting. That dog meant everything to her.

'I can give him an injection to put him to sleep.' Sarah was a professional, but still there was sadness in her wise eyes. 'It'll be painless, I assure you. You can stay with him till the end, if you like.'

Judith nodded again and sank down on the chair that Sarah pushed behind her knees.

Once more, she took Bertie's paw in her hand and gently stroked his head. His eyes looked into hers, full of love and trust, and pleading.

Sarah went out of the room, tactfully giving Judith a few minutes to be with Bertie before the final act. When she came back, she had a syringe in her hand. Judith looked at it and gulped audibly.

'Are you ready?' Sarah asked gently,

and Judith nodded.

'Goodbye, sweetheart,' she whispered and felt the dog jerk slightly as the needle sank in. 'I won't ever forget you.'

'I'm sure he knows that,' Sarah said, her hand again on Judith's shoulder as they watched the dog's eyes gradually close and heard his long, last sigh.

11

It was Rory who dug a grave in his own garden, next to the grave of his old spaniel, Jasper. He wouldn't allow Judith to look until the grave was covered over, then he left her alone to weep for her beloved Bertie in private.

An hour later, when she was sitting on a bench in the sun, looking at the leaves and flowers dripping the last dregs of the storm, Rory came out carrying a couple of large whiskies and handed her one.

'In the middle of the afternoon?' she queried, her face creasing into a reluctant smile, shamefully aware that her eyes were swollen and red-rimmed. 'What will people say?'

'I don't much care, do you? I think we deserve a drop of the hard stuff after all we've been through.'

Judith took a sip of the whisky, glad

to find it was mixed with a large amount of ginger wine.

'Oh, that's good, but I don't want to get drunk on it. My head's not too used to strong alcohol.'

'Don't worry. I don't take advantage of the situation, I promise.'

He was smiling, but his eyes were still dark and serious, so she wasn't sure if he was joking or not.

'Is Fred really going to be all right?' she said, clearing her throat noisily and turning to inspect a red rose glistening with diamante raindrops.

'It would appear so,' Rory said, drinking his whisky and staring off into the middle distance. 'We really ought to do something about accommodation for him, but he's not an easy man to deal with. None of them are. They don't like to be pinned down.'

'Tramps?' she said, 'Or just men in general?'

'Glad to see you're feeling better!'

It would be a long time before she got over losing Bertie, but she wasn't the type to wear her sadness on her sleeve. She was sensible enough to know that life went on and it was possible to smile, no matter what suffering you hid inside.

At least nobody had made the remark that Bertie was just a dog, after all. She would have torn them apart if they had. Bertie, unlike the men in her life so far, had given her fifteen years of unconditional love. That kind of thing was difficult to replace.

'What makes people like Fred turn to a life on the road?' she asked, trying to keep her thoughts on a less personal plain.

'There's a question now. We all have our little secrets hidden so deep inside us that sometimes even we don't understand them.'

'Are you speaking about yourself, Rory?'

He stared into his glass and she heard a sharp intake of breath before he lifted it to his lips and drained it in one long gulp.

'I had a long talk with my son before he left for university,' he said, quite out of the blue. 'He'd told me he'd been to see you.'

'Yes. He said that you had forbidden him to see me,' she told him. 'Why was that?'

There was the hint of a shrug, and his attention remained in the bottom of his empty glass.

'To be honest, Ben is forever trying to fix me up with some woman or other. I suppose I feel that in some way he's betraying his mother. He was so young when she died, and she'd been sick for a long time before that. He was raised by his granny. I don't think he remembers Laura all that well, really.'

'And you? Do you feel that you're betraying your dead wife?'

'What?' He scrutinised her through half-closed eyes, then he seemed to know where she was coming from. 'With Sarah, do you mean? Sarah and I have been good friends since I was a kid. She was the one who inspired me to become a vet. She taught me all she knew. When Laura became ill, Sarah was my rock.' He suddenly did a double take as a thought occurred to him. 'You didn't think I was having an affair with her, did you?'

Judith felt cornered. Of course she thought that, but the idea had been put in her head by Maggie, who had been so sure of her facts.

'Does it matter what I think?' she said, trying to make light of it. 'Your life is your own, Rory.'

'Yes, I know, but . . . well, I'm not . . . never have had . . . ' He frowned and his face twisted as he struggled with his words. 'Besides, she's at least fifteen years older than me. I love her to bits, but that's it.'

Judith wasn't going to fall into the trap of asking him anything else. It would make it look as if she were interested, which she wasn't.

Well, that's what she kept telling herself, even though he was the most attractive man she had ever met. And she was staying in his house, unbelievable though that may seem.

She had only agreed to stay because the local hotels were full of tourists, and storm-bedraggled campers. And Ben was expected home for half term, so it seemed to make it all right.

She could have refused Rory's offer, of course, but it would have seemed rude to do so after all he had done for her. Besides, she could hardly have told him that she couldn't stay because she was afraid of getting involved. How would that have looked to him.

Rory was on his feet. He raised his glass. 'I'm going to have another one. How about you?'

She shook her head, tempted to ask if he was being wise, but then he seemed to be responsible enough to know what he was doing. With a bit of luck he wouldn't be called out to another emergency that day, animal or human.

A few minutes later, he was back with her, but wandered restlessly to and fro in front of her, his long legs travelling the ground in slow, deliberate strides.

Then he halted, his back to her, elbows tucked in to his sides. Even without seeing his expression, she knew that he was experiencing some kind of stress and his next words proved it.

'When our daughter was killed, Laura blamed me,' he said suddenly. 'That's pretty hard to live with, you know. It was hard for both of us at the time. You know the kind of thing. If I had shut the gate properly behind me, Katie wouldn't have wandered out on to the road. And if Laura hadn't closed the front door, or checked the gate, same thing. And if that motorist had not driven too fast on a foggy morning . . . '

His head swivelled around and Judith saw the pain of the memories reflected in his eyes, then he was continuing and she let him talk, feeling that he needed the release it would give him.

'We tried to patch things up between us, but it was mainly an act to fool the public. It never really fooled us. I still loved her, but what we had had together was dead. We even talked about divorce. Ironically enough, the day I made my decision to put an end to the marriage, she discovered she was pregnant with Ben. And a few weeks later, she was diagnosed with cancer.'

'That must have been a very difficult time for you,' Judith said, draining her whisky and feeling very glad of it.

'It was. I was riddled with guilt. Sarah took me under her wing. I don't know what I would have done without her.'

'And all these years later?' Judith said. 'Do you still feel guilty about the whole thing?'

'Now? I feel guilty in a different way,' Rory sat down and rubbed a hand over his face. 'You see, Judith, I can't even remember Laura's face unless I look at her photograph. I think I can remember her voice — and sometimes I think I can hear my little girl's laughter. Other than that, it's just a big empty void.'

'So why do you get irritated when

Ben tries to encourage you to see other women? Surely that's a good sign, that he can think like that.'

'Maybe,' Rory said, then dropped his face into his hands and groaned. 'I think he has ulterior motives because of the girl he's besotted with. As for me, the very idea of taking up with another woman has never appealed to me. I've had too many near misses.'

'I don't understand,' Judith said.

Rory gave a short laugh. 'Oh, Judith, you'd be amazed at how many women hit on us poor widower types. We bring out the maternal instincts in some. Others think, mistakenly, that we are just desperate for a replacement wife.'

'I see,' Judith said, mentally drawing a blue biro line through the name of Dr Rory Telford. 'Well, you don't have anything to worry about from me, because I can't think of anything worse than taking on another man. Not after a bad marriage and a messy divorce. I'm quite happy as I am, thank you very much.'

He looked up, surprise registering on his face.

'I'm glad to hear it,' he said. 'I assume, that being the case, that we can actually be friends.'

'Yes, of course,' she said. 'No problem.'

And she meant it. Of course she meant it — didn't she?

12

It was inevitable that Maggie and George would come at the gallop when they heard what had happened. By the time they arrived, Judith was back in the van, happy with her re-found solitude and just as happy to leave Rory with his, despite thoughts of him invading her mind when she was least expecting it.

'So what happened, exactly?' Maggie wanted to know as the two women sat in the recovering rose garden with a bottle of Chardonnay between them, while George did a tour of inspection, noting the damage caused by the storm.

'Well, it lasted for hours,' Judith told her, drinking deeply as she recalled the horrific events of that night.

'It must have been frightening for you, dear.'

'There was too much to think about

to be frightened, Maggie. I just went from one horror to the next like a zombie.'

'And you lost poor little Bertie,' Maggie's chin quivered with emotion and Judith turned away, because it would be a long time before she could think of that dog without shedding a tear or two.

'At least the poor blighter had a good innings,' George said, overhearing the conversation. 'And you say that big conifer of ours crushed your car, Judith?'

'Yes,' Judith got up and joined him where he stood, staring at the bare patch of earth where the tree had been uprooted. 'The local farmer came and took it away and the garage have loaned me one of their cars until I get the insurance sorted out and buy a new one.'

George surveyed the whole hillside and shook his head in disbelief.

'This whole ruddy planet is chang-ing,' he said grumpily. 'It's the global warming, that's what it is. We're all guilty, you know. Every last one of us. Polluting the air with chemicals and God knows what. Let's go back to the good old horse and cart, that's what I say.'

Maggie came to stand with them, putting a glass of wine in her husband's hand with a fond smile.

'That's not what he used to say when he lived on his parents' old farm and there wasn't any public transport for miles around. Isn't that right, George? Always complaining at how slow things moved.'

'Och, aye, but then I was always in a hurry to get somewhere. At my advanced age there's nowhere to go except the cemetery and I'm in no hurry for that, I can tell you.'

The women laughed and Judith felt her spirits lift for the first time in days.

'So, did you stay here in the van or did you have to take a room at the tavern in the village?' Maggie asked.

Judith contemplated lying to her

friends, but thought better of it. Liars, she firmly believed, were invariably found out sooner or later, unless they were very, very good. And she was a hopeless liar. She took after her grandmother, who always maintained that one should tell the truth and shame the devil.

'Actually, Maggie, I stayed at the Telford place, but just for a couple of nights.'

'Really? Didn't you stay with him once before?' Maggie was doing her best not to look reproachful, but she couldn't hide the look of suspicion in her eyes.

'Yes, I did. If you remember, it was when I first arrived and there was the first storm.'

'Looks like the weather is plotting against you, lassie,' George said with a chuckle. 'Or is it working in favour of the good vet of Merrivale.'

'George!' Maggie clicked her tongue at him, then turned back to Judith. 'Seriously, Judith, there's nothing going on between you and Dr Telford, is there?'

Judith shook her head. 'Nothing at all, Maggie,' she said and was surprised to feel an uncomfortable fluttering rise from her stomach to her ribcage. 'He was just a kind samaritan, who probably regretted being in the wrong place at the right time.'

'How do you figure that?' George was in one of his inquisitive moods and Judith felt a third-degree questioning coming on. 'I would have thought that he'd welcome having an attractive young woman under his roof, after years of being a widower.'

'Yes,' Maggie sighed. 'Such a tragic case, that, by all accounts, but there is that other woman. I don't suppose you know if he's still seeing her?'

'If you mean Sarah Carlisle, they're just good friends. Anyway, she's years older than Rory.'

Maggie gave her a wry smile. 'And that makes it all right, does it? Do be careful, my dear. Don't be fooled by that charm of his. He already has a bit of a reputation around here by all accounts. I wouldn't want you to be added to his list of conquests.'

'Maggie!' Judith suppressed a sudden ride of irritation. 'The man is single and attractive and probably lonely for companionship, just as you would be — if you lost George.'

'Oh, no, Judith. I couldn't contemplate another man in my life. Not after George.'

'Maggie, Maggie . . . ' George came to the rescue. 'I'm very flattered by your loyalty, but Judith here is still young and she deserves to find somebody else.'

'Exactly, George,' Judith said in her own defence. 'And maybe I will, one day, but I'm not ready yet, and when I am, it won't be Rory Telford because . . . because . . . '

'Yes, dear?'

'Well, he's not interested, that's why. He's made that perfectly clear and . . . well, I'm not that kind to throw myself at just any man. I have too much pride for that.'

Both Maggie and George looked at her from beneath lowered brows and she groaned inwardly as she realised that they were thinking exactly what she had been telling herself since the day she arrived at Merrivale. She was protesting too much.

13

'Oh, I'm so pleased you came to see me, Judith!' Mrs Barrett was, as usual, up to her elbows in flour as she pounded a lump of elastic bread dough on the heavy oak slab that was her kitchen table as well as her baking board. Her rosy cheeks dimpled at the sight of Judith. She wiped her hands down her apron and pulled out a chair.

'Thank you, Mrs Barrett,' Judith said, sitting down and inhaling with obvious pleasure the odours of the kitchen. 'Oh, it always smells so good here.'

'Aye, lass.' Mrs Barrett rolled down her sleeves, all the while regarding her visitor, an expectant smile on her face. 'So, you've been having adventures, I heard, you and Rory Telford.'

'Well, I wouldn't call it that,' Judith said, colouring slightly.

'No, it can't have been pleasant for

you finding old Fred like that. I hear he's going to be all right. Eeh, that man! If he fell into a heap of manure he'd come up smelling of violets.'

'I like him, actually,' Judith said. 'He's done a lot to help me while I've been here and he never takes advantage.'

'Oh, don't get me wrong, Judith,' Mrs Barrett gave an infectious laugh. 'He's harmless. He has a problem relating to people, that's all. You're honoured the way he's taken to you. Most of the time he shies away from any kind of contact. And he's not the only one around here with that problem, either.'

Judith concentrated on the dough and wished Mrs Barrett would continue thumping it and they could talk of unimportant things, anything but what she knew was going through the older woman's mind. She had called in on Mrs Barrett because she felt so lonely now that she didn't have Bertie to keep her company.

'My friends,' she said, hoping to change the subject, 'Maggie and George . . . they came to see me the other day.'

'Aye, I heard. I also heard that your poor dog died. Sorry to hear that. It's always hard to lose an animal like that. He was a nice looking dog, too.'

'Please, could we talk about something else?' Judith pleaded.

'You should get yourself another dog, love. The sooner the better.'

'Yes. One day, but . . . '

'Rory tells me he buried your Bertie next to Jasper in his garden. That's cosy, I thought.'

'Cosy?'

'Well, you and him . . . Rory, I mean.'

'Oh, but . . . Mrs Barrett, it's not like that . . . '

But Mrs Barrett carried on, regardless. 'I saw the way he looked at you that first day you were here and I said to my Harry, I said, there's romance brewing for Dr Telford.'

'No! Mrs Barrett, I can't let you go on like this,' Judith objected. 'Really, there's nothing like that between us.'

Mrs Barrett's head jerked round and she fixed a beady eye on Judith that said she knew more than she was prepared to let on.

'Well, if there isn't love, there ought to be, that's all I can say.'

'Oh, dear,' Judith sank low in her seat and groaned. 'First Ben, now you. And you're both wrong you know.'

'Are you going to tell me, Judith, that you don't find Rory Telford attractive?'

'Yes . . . I mean, no.' Judith felt a hot flush creep up from her neck to her hairline. 'No, actually, I find him very attractive, but . . . '

'Aye?'

'He's made it perfectly clear that he wants nothing to do with any woman . . . especially me, I suspect.'

Judith saw Mrs Bennett's gaze shift to the space behind her left shoulder and she jumped guiltily as she heard the scuff of a shoe on the stone flag floor. Twisting around in her chair, she gasped in embarrassment at the sight of

Rory Telford entering the room.

'Well, speak of the devil,' Mrs Bennett said and gave a loud guffaw of laughter. 'What can I do for you today, Dr Telford?'

Rory cleared his throat and looked from one woman to the other, his eyes wider than usual, his expression one of affected indifference at having walked in on an intimate conversation, of which he was the subject.

'I just stopped by with a supply of vitamins for Samson,' he said quickly, placing a pharmacy box on the table next to where Judith was still sitting. 'Good morning, Judith. I trust everything's all right up at the van?'

'Thank you, yes. Everything's fine.' Judith stood up slowly and pushed her chair back. 'I was just going.'

'Och, lassie,' Mrs Bennett objected. 'You've only just arrived. Now sit down, the pair of you, and we'll have a cup of coffee together. There's fresh apple turnovers just out of the oven and I know how you like them, Rory.'

'Yes, but I . . . ' He was meeting Judith's embarrassed gaze with one of his own. 'I have a heavy schedule before me this morning. I should be getting on.'

'And I promised I'd visit Fred in the hospital,' Judith said, deciding that now was the perfect time to do so.

'Now that's a coincidence,' Mrs Barrett's voice was quite matter-of-fact, but Judith suspected an ulterior motive in there somewhere. 'Rory, I seem to remember you telling me you were going into the hospital this morning, too. You can take Judith with you, and take old Fred some of those apple turnovers . . . after you've sampled them yourselves, of course. Now, is it white coffee or black?'

★   ★   ★

'I really am sorry about this,' Judith said with a sigh as she sat beside Rory in his jeep on the way to the hospital.

'It wasn't your fault, Judith,' he said

with a wry smile. 'Doris Barrett's a strong-willed woman when she wants to be. Besides, it makes sense the two of us travelling together into town. And I'm sure Fred will appreciate the visit.'

Judith shrugged and studied his hands on the steering wheel. They were such big, strong, capable hands. They were the kind of hands that made a woman feel safe.

She gave a shudder as she had a fleeting thought of those same hands touching her. But that's all it was. Fleeting. She couldn't afford to dream any further than that. Rory Telford had been emasculated by the deaths of his daughter and his wife. If he was looking for solace, he certainly wasn't looking her way.

As they parked in the visitors' car park outside the General Hospital, Rory fell strangely silent. He made no effort to get out of the jeep and sat there, fingers tapping the wheel, the muscle in his cheek flexing.

'Did you mean what you said back

there in Doris Barrett's kitchen?' he said, taking her by surprise. 'About finding me attractive?'

Judith felt her heart trip. She drew in a deep breath and licked her lips before letting it out slowly.

'You weren't supposed to hear that,' she said, her mouth forcing itself into a wry smile. 'You know what women are like when they get on to the subject of men.'

'So you don't find me attractive?'

'I didn't say that.' Judith stumbled over her words, then gave him a sidelong glance. 'Actually you are very attractive, but then you know that already.'

'Do I?'

'Yes, of course you do.'

'Judith, if I asked you to . . . '

'Shall we go and see Fred?' Judith asked swiftly, not giving him the chance to finish his sentence. 'I have a million and one things to do today and I really can't waste time discussing how good looking you are, Rory.'

She saw him blink and when he took the keys out of the ignition it was the abrupt action of an angry man. Judith felt like kicking herself, but the last thing she wanted was to give him the impression that she was chasing him.

She had no intention of joining the long list of also-rans in his little black book of women who tried and failed to trap Rory Telford into a relationship they would both end up regretting.

14

With autumn well under way and winter just around the corner, the social life in the village started to pick up. Judith found she was the receiver of rather more invitations to dine out than she felt she could comfortably cope with. But it wasn't easy turning people down, and she didn't want to hurt any feelings, since this was their way of accepting her in their midst.

And, of course, it filled the lonely hours with friendly faces and impersonal conversation. The big drawback, from Judith's point of view, was the number of times that Rory Telford was also present. But then, it was a small village and the vet was well known because everyone, without exception had need of his professional expertise. It was only natural they should invite him.

When they did come face to face, he was cool but polite. She decided that he was still suffering from the blow to his ego that she had delivered by not showing interest in him as a man. Or was she being a mite too conceited. He probably didn't find her in the least attractive and, judging by the women who so frequently draped themselves all over him in public, there was no shortage of likely candidates for his affections.

Ben had not come home at half term after all. He had telephoned to say that he was going to spend his first time off from university with his girlfriend's parents. The news had thrown Rory into a black mood, which affected everybody.

Judith had been looking forward to seeing the boy again. He had sent her a very sweet letter of condolence over the death of Bertie. Added, as a postscript, was a sentence that had both surprised and amused her. *Please keep an eye on Dad for me and save him from himself.*

'What's putting that smile on your face?'

Judith's head snapped around and she gulped to find Rory standing next to her chair, bending down low so he could whisper in her ear. It was the occasion of the Barretts' golden wedding party in the church hall and it seemed that the whole village was there.

'Rory! Actually, I was just thinking of Ben and wondering how he's getting on.'

'He's getting on his father's nerves,' was the snappy reply, then Rory's expression softened. 'Oh, I know I'm being hard on the lad, but I don't want him to make any big mistakes that he'll spend a lifetime regretting.'

'You can't go on forever trying to live his life for him, Rory,' she said. 'From what I saw of him, Ben's a sensible, responsible adult. You've done a good job raising him. Maybe it's time to back off and let him breathe on his own.'

'Thank you for your expert opinion.'

'I know I'm not a parent,' she said,

smarting from his criticism. 'But I've been a child and an adolescent and a teenager and I can tell you, it's not easy relating to parents. And that is my expert opinion.'

Rory pulled out the chair beside her that was temporarily vacant, her neighbour having gone to prop up the bar and eye the younger female talent.

'Do you mind if I join you?'

'Feel free.' She hoped he wasn't attaching himself to her because there were no other available females. Or worse, taking pity on her.

'You're looking particularly lovely this evening, Judith,' he said.

Oh, goodness, she sighed inwards. Where did he get that old line from? If he was going to go on like that she would definitely go home. She had been on the point of doing so anyway, but she hated returning alone to the cold, empty van with no welcoming bark and wag of a feathery tail, no pink tongue to lick her fingers as she fondled his ears. Oh, dear, she must stop thinking of

Bertie or she would cry.

'It's been a nice party,' she said through clenched jaws, blinking away the tears that threatened to spill.

'It's great to think that some marriages do last the test of time,' Rory said, then suddenly his hand closed over hers and she felt his fingers grip. 'Come on. They're playing the last dance and you haven't danced all night.'

'Oh, but I don't . . . ' She started to object, but he was pulling her to her feet. To resist would attract more attention than just going mildly with him on to the dance floor.

It was old-fashioned music and an old-fashioned waltz and neither of them were adept with the steps, but they compromised and got around the floor without too much trouble.

'I'd almost forgotten what it was like to dance like this,' Rory said into the top of her head and she tried desperately not to enjoy too much the feel of his arms around her.

'You could have fooled me,' she said, keeping the conversation light. 'I saw you enjoying yourself earlier.'

'Jiving with the brassy blonde?'

'And the raunchy redhead. Not to mention the buxom brunette.'

His body jerked spasmodically and his feet faltered, making him tread on her toes. Judith looked up to find him laughing.

'And what category are you in, Judith?'

'I don't think I'm in their league,' she told him stiffly and then apologised when she almost tripped him.

'No, you're not, thank goodness.' He slowed down and stopped dancing, though the band played on. 'Judith, I can almost hear your thoughts and, believe me, you're totally wrong about me. I'm not, as you seem to believe, some kind of Lakeland playboy working his amoral way through the women of Cumbria.'

'I don't see how it concerns me what you do with your life, Rory.'

'Don't you? In that case, maybe I was mistaken about you.'

They stood there, in the middle of the dance floor, with couples gyrating around them. Suddenly, it seemed to Judith that the music had faded and so had the other dancers. All she was aware of was Rory's arms around her and his dark eyes penetrating her senses, and violating her soul.

He bent his head, so that his face came close to hers. Too close. He placed the lightest butterfly kiss on her forehead, then another on her cheek.

'You really do look lovely tonight,' he whispered, and it made her throat tighten. 'I know it's a hackneyed phrase, but I'm the old-fashioned type and I don't know how else to tell you the truth.'

'Please, Rory,' she hissed back at him, her eyes flying about the room as sound and reality came back to her ears. 'People are looking.'

'Let them look. They're my friends, Judith. Yours too, if you'll let them into your tight little world.'

'I think I'd better go now,' she told him pushing him away with arms that felt as weak as rubber.

'Let me take you . . . '

'No!'

'At least let me walk you to your car.'

'Your friends will miss you.'

Judith was marching out of the hall, grabbing her bag on the way, forgetting her coat, forgetting to say goodnight to the Barretts or any of the villagers she now knew. She felt hot and angry and close to tears so it was important to leave quickly before she made an absolute fool of herself.

'Judith, wait . . . please!'

He was there at her elbow as she hurried across the car park. She fumbled with her keys and couldn't get the door open. In one overpowering move, Rory took hold of her and swung her around. The keys fell to the ground.

'Don't!' she said, aware that the moonlight was shining down on them and he would see the glisten of tears on her lashes. 'Please, don't.'

'I have to,' he said softly, then his mouth was on hers and she felt as if the whole world had turned on its axis, making her giddy.

She had never been kissed like that before. Not even by her husband during those years when she thought she was madly in love, only to find that it was an illusion. This feeling she had for Rory Telford was no illusion. It was deep and profound, and very, very scary.

They separated abruptly as the door to the church hall rattled open and people started pouring out. One or two smiled and nodded at the slightly breathless couple.

Judith could sense Rory's irritation at being disturbed, and his impatience to continue. It was mad to get mixed up with another man so soon after the divorce, and the last thing she wanted right now.

'I must go,' Judith said, scooping up the keys from the ground at her feet.

'Wait!' He tried to catch hold of her, but she escaped his searching hands and jumped into her car. 'Judith, please don't rush off like this. We have to talk.'

She shook her head at him through the closed window of the car door, but couldn't bring herself to speak.

Thankfully, the engine started easily and she was soon driving up the hill, her headlights picking out the trees like ghostly creatures of the night with long, tangled arms waving a warning to her to be careful.

15

The next few days were difficult for Judith. She started off by a visit to the Barretts, where she gave abject apologies to Doris for fleeing the scene of the party without a word. Mrs Barrett just smiled safely, saying she had been too overwhelmed by the evening to even notice.

Judith knew that wasn't quite true, but she was grateful that the woman didn't make a fuss or get offended by her bizarre behaviour. But then, after a few minutes, during which Doris produced tea and hot cheese scones dripping with butter, she fixed Judith with a beady, enquiring eye.

'So why did you run off like that? You were dancing so nicely with Rory. It did my heart good to see the pair of you dancing together like that.'

'It was only a dance, Doris. Nothing special.'

'He couldn't keep his eyes off you all night. Don't think I didn't notice.'

Judith took a scone and concentrated on eating it without the butter dripping down her chin.

'Anyway, did you enjoy your anniversary party, Doris?' she asked in a loud, unsteady voice, hoping to change the subject.

'Aye, it was lovely, though me corns are throbbing this morning and Harry's still in bed complaining that he's danced his back out of kilter.'

Judith smiled broadly, remembering how the elderly couple had been on the floor for every dance and put the younger guests to shame.

'Maybe you should do it more often.'

'Och, get away with you, girl. The older you are the longer it takes to recover from such things. I think we've reached an age when our enjoyment needs to come from quieter pursuits.'

Quieter pursuits. Judith sighed, thinking that she was finally getting restless and bored living a life of solitude in the static van with only a rose garden to keep her busy and a few books to read in the long, lonely evenings. Perhaps, at last, she was recovering her normal vitality and it was time to do something about it.

'I don't think I'll be staying too much longer,' she told Doris, who raised an eyebrow and pursed her lips.

'You're not thinking of leaving us, are you, Judith? Why, girl, you're one of us now.'

'Oh, Doris, I don't know. I love it here, but I can't live in a static van for the rest of my life, and I really have to find myself a job. I'm starting to vegetate.'

'A job is it? Well, you can probably find one around here if you look hard enough. I may even know of one that you would be eminently suitable for. How about that, eh?'

'What? Where?' Judith felt a rise of enthusiasm flame through her, then she slumped in her chair and reached for another scone. 'Oh, but I really need to find more permanent accommodation. Maggie and George's van has done me proud, but . . . '

'I know what you mean, but I might be able to help you find a proper place of your own too. Leave it with me for a wee while, eh?'

They left it like that. And as the days rolled by, Judith was more and more sure that she couldn't continue the way she was. She was becoming hyperactive and twitchy and positively irritable. It was a clear sign that she was coming out of the post-divorce rut. It was time to move on.

It was ten days since the party and she had not seen hide nor hair of Rory Telford. Again, Judith had mixed feelings about the situation. Part of her was glad that he had not bothered her since being rebuffed. The other, less sensible part of her longed to see him again and didn't care if he was the local gigolo.

If only she could just once more experience those strong arms holding her, and that kiss that had upset her equilibrium to such an extent she felt that no other kiss could ever match it.

She was resting her eyes after a long period of reading when someone rattled the door of the van. It was raining again, but not the torrential rain of the storm, which had done so much destruction around the valley. This was a gentle, soothing rain and she quite liked to hear it tapping on the metal roof and running off it in musical streams, bouncing on pots, and plopping into puddles.

'Hello?'

She sat up hastily as she recognised Rory's voice hailing her, and wondered if she could get away with pretending she wasn't there. Almost before she discarded this idea she was on her feet and pulling open the door, gazing down at his upturned face beneath the hood of his anorak. An autumn chill swept into the van and she shivered convulsively.

'Rory! What are you doing here?'

'You'd better let me come in or you'll lose all your heat,' he said casually as if he hadn't noticed the embarrassment his presence was causing. 'A few minutes of your time is all I'm asking.'

It would have been idiotic to argue. After all, she was the one who had behaved badly the last time she had seen him. Perhaps he had come for an explanation. She certainly owed him one, for after some reflection on the matter, Judith had decided that she had behaved like a stupid schoolgirl receiving her first adult kiss and not knowing how to cope with it.

'All right,' she said, stepping back from the door and allowing him to pass inside.

He unzipped his anorak, pushing the hood free of his head and glanced quickly around him. She was about to speak, trying to formulate some kind of bland apology that would not lead to anything other than an equally bland acceptance. But he forestalled her.

'Judith, I'm sorry it's taken so long,

but here I am and I want to apologise to you.' He threw his arms wide and regarded her with arched eyebrows and dark, sincere eyes. 'I was completely out of place the other night. My behaviour plainly upset you, which was the last thing I wanted to do. The fact was, I had drunk too much, and I wasn't entirely responsible for my actions. Will you please forgive me?'

Judith swallowed hard. Oh, dear. This was so difficult. How could a woman be 'just friends' with a man who affected her so physically? His face, his voice, haunted her every waking hour as if he had taken up permanent residence in her mind.

'Of course I can,' she said, easing the tension in her shoulders as she wondered what else she could say.

'That's good, because I have a favour to ask of you.'

'Oh?'

'Yes. Doris Barrett tells me that you're thinking of finding somewhere permanent to live and . . . well, she says you'd quite like to stay in the area as long as you can find a job.'

'Yes, that's true, but . . . '

'Now, wait till I've finished, and then you can have time to think it over.'

'Think what over?'

'I'm transferring my surgery to Sarah's place. It's bigger and more central and since I can call on Sarah to help out when things get busy, it makes perfect sense, don't you think?'

Judith could only think of Rory moving in with Sarah, nice attractive woman, older woman. She said nothing and let him continue.

'Anyway, I thought of renting out my cottage. It's tiny, but cosy enough and I would charge you a peppercorn rent if . . . '

'If?' Judith held her breath, not daring to add her own version on the end of that one small word.

'If you would agree to come and work for me as my assistant, secretary . . . no matter what. I really need someone to keep me straight on the paperwork and to help out occasionally in the surgery. Sarah and I would train you, of course.'

She stared at him, not believing her ears. Her heart thumped warningly in her chest and she had to walk up and down the van because she needed to keep moving, otherwise she would freeze.

'Oh, Rory, I don't know . . . '

'How about if we have a six-month trial period. See how we get along?'

Judith shook her head and saw the disappointment in his face, felt the heavy stone of disappointment sink in her own stomach.

'It's a very generous offer, but . . . ' How could she possibly accept?

'Think about it,' he insisted, then he was suddenly running back to his car and the gentle rain was not so gentle any more.

16

'So when do you want me to start?'
Judith didn't mean to make it sound so
brusque, but she was nervous, having
gone ahead and done the very thing she
swore she would never do. She had
accepted Rory Telford's offer after a
long, heart to heart chat with Doris
Barrett. And it was a generous offer.
The salary wasn't exactly to die for, but
there was the cottage to be taken into
consideration and it was the kind of
work she knew she would enjoy.

'Just as soon as you stop frowning at
me,' Rory said with a lop-sided smile.
'I've already moved the practice and my
personal belongings out of the cottage.
I suggest you put up with my old
furniture until you decide whether or
not you're going to stay.'

'Or whether or not you still want me
after six months,' she told firmly.

'We'll see. Anyway, take a day or two to get settled into the place, then Sarah will take charge of you until you're confident enough to know what you're doing.'

Judith nodded. Each time he mentioned Sarah, her stomach did a back flip and she cursed herself for being so inadequate that she couldn't accept the fact that the most attractive man in the world was living with a woman almost old enough to be his mother. And this after indicating that the woman was merely a good friend. How shallow men could be.

Come on, come on, Judith! She tossed her head and stuck her chin out resolutely. You're a mature, fully-grown woman. Suddenly you've got a job and a dream cottage in a place you've always wanted to live. Don't let a good-looking man with shaky morals stand in your way.

She knew that once she could accept Rory for what he was, she would be able to close the door on her infatuation, if

136

that's what it was, and settle down to her new life. And who knows? One day, she might even meet someone she would actually like to spend the rest of her life with.

Fat chance! She heard the voice in her head and shook herself free of it. Take a couple of days, he had said. Well, the sooner she started the better.

'Is it all right if I choose new curtains and stuff?' she asked. 'Make the place more . . . ' She hesitated, hoping he wasn't going to be insulted, 'More me?'

'Go ahead,' he said convivially. 'I never did like those curtains anyway. The cottage is dark. It needs brightening up. I'm sure you will know how to do that more efficiently than I ever could.'

'Thanks,' she said, surprised that her smile was full and genuine.

'Enjoy yourself.' He reached for his coat and the pile of veterinary magazines he had stashed by the door, the last remnants of his personal effects, and gave her a brief nod before making his exit.

Judith waited until she heard the car engine start up, then she spun around and beamed at her new home. It was going to be so much fun making the place her own. There wouldn't be time to dwell on the loss of her beloved dog. Even so, Bertie's remains were only in the back garden. She would plant some rosemary over his grave.

And she would be far too busy to spare a thought of what might have been had Dr Rory Telford been . . . well, different. By Monday, she would have the cottage, and her head, sorted out. And she would do her best to like Sarah, even if she didn't approve of her.

* * *

'Well, Judith, I don't think there's anything left to cover right now,' Sarah said.

She had perched on the end of Judith's desk. They had just finished going over the filing system and the appointments book. Everything seemed pretty straightforward up to this point. The rest would fall into place gradually.

'Thank you. It's very good of you to give up your time to show me the ropes.'

'Nonsense. Rory deserves the best help he can get, but he doesn't have time to spend too long in the office. The least I can do is train you. I know the job backwards. And I know Rory.'

'Yes,' Judith said meekly and saw the other woman scrutinise her closely.

'Judith, forgive me for being blunt, but I'm too old to pussyfoot about. I detect a certain reticence in you that bothers me.'

'No, really, it's nothing . . . '

'Sure about that?' Sarah raised an eyebrow and smiled a little too knowingly for Judith's comfort. 'As a matter of fact, I was surprised that Rory took you on.'

Judith stared at her. 'Why do you say that?'

Sarah slid her behind off the desk

and went to replace a file in the filing cabinet where all the old records still resided. One of Judith's first priorities would be to transfer these records on to the computer.

'Put it this way.' Sarah remained by the cabinet, staring into hits contents. 'Rory doesn't usually mix business with pleasure.'

'I don't know what you mean by that, Sarah,' Judith said slowly.

'He told me how he blew it with you, Judith.'

Judith's eyes widened as she tried to grasp what Sarah was trying to say. She could only be speaking of that memorable moment with Rory at the Barrett's anniversary party.

'You're going to have to be more specific than that,' Judith said, aware of a sudden prickly heat attacking her arms and rushing up to her cheeks.

'Rory doesn't make a habit of running after woman, though none of us could blame him if he did after so many years on his own.' Sarah turned to face Judith. 'You seemed to be the exception and we all applauded it.'

'But . . . ' Judith was more than a little confused and the creases in her forehead showed it. 'I thought that you . . . and he . . . After all, you've living together, aren't you?'

Sarah threw her head back and laughed loudly. 'Oh, my dear, how amusing! You don't mean to say that you've been fighting Rory off because you thought he was being unfaithful to me?'

The colour drained from Judith's face. She felt humiliated before this woman who was so much more worldly wise than she would ever be.

'What was I supposed to think?'

Sarah heaved a great sigh of exasperation and shook her head. 'Judith, Rory is like the son I never had. I adore him, but the thought of any romantic entanglement with him is preposterous to me. When you came to Merrivale, I saw some life come back into that man's eyes and I wasn't the only one.

We were all keeping our fingers crossed that you were the one to get to his heart. And I think you did, but then everything changed. What happened?'

Judith swallowed with difficulty and wasn't quite sure how to respond.

'It wasn't Rory who messed up, Sarah,' she said eventually. 'It was me. I thought he was no better than the other men in my life. I didn't want to be made a fool of yet again, or get hurt. One minute he was treating me with ill-mannered indifference, the next he was coming on to me and ... I was wrong, wasn't I?'

'I think the pair of you were wrong and, if you ask me, you both need your heads banging together, but I'm not going to interfere. I've already said enough on the subject.'

Sarah went to the door and stood there, hesitantly, obviously struggling with the tangle of thoughts in her head.

'I almost wish you hadn't told me,' Judith said glumly, feeling her emotions tying themselves in knots that were even tighter than before.

'I don't usually blab, but I hate to see two lovely people, who are obviously made for one another, miss out because they're too stubborn or too blind to see what's happening.'

'I see.'

'And, for your information, we do not live together. I live upstairs and Rory has a tiny apartment under the roof. He doesn't sleep well. I hear him moving about all night.'

'Oh?'

'Which is why I was surprised he hired you rather than let you leave. Ah, well, there's no accounting for some people.'

'No,' Judith said, not sure she understood that last remark. 'No, there isn't.'

It was strange the way things worked out. Strange and very convenient, Judith thought. The practice was experiencing an unusually quiet period, so she found Rory coming into the office rather than haring about the countryside delivering breach births, treating mastitis and generally coddling the local farming community.

However, the quiet period allowed her to observe her new boss very closely and she soon realised how much she had ruined things by spurning him the way she had. But at least he had not held a grudge and they seemed to get along fine, and that was something. It would never go beyond that now, she was sure, but one day she was going to be able to put her regrets behind her, just as he obviously had.

'Any calls?' Rory's head appeared around the door, and when she told him 'no', he looked relieved. 'In that case, I'll catch up on my paperwork.'

They had adjoining desks. He used a laptop rather than the main computer that she sat in front of. If she happened to go to his side of the office, he would make sure she didn't see what he was tapping away at. However, she knew, having been told on the side by Sarah, that he was working on a book. It was, she had confided with a broad smile, the tales of a fictitious vet, though the anecdotes were true enough.

'How's it going?' Judith asked casually when he had been staring into space for some minutes.

'What?'

'The book.' She nodded towards the laptop, which he swiftly closed and frowned down at the lid, then at her.

'You're not supposed to know about that,' he said.

'Why not? I think it's wonderful that you actually have something to occupy your time other than saving the lives of animals.'

He continued to stare at the laptop, his fingers tapping on the desk.

'It fills in the hours,' he said, giving her a quizzical look. 'How do you fill in your spare time?'

'I read and walk a lot,' she told him.

'I used to enjoy walking over the hills when Jasper was alive. It's perfect for emptying the head and sorting out problems.'

'Yes, I know what you mean. Unfortunately, once Bertie lost his leg, we gave up our long rambles together. It was never the same on my own.'

'Well, in that case, maybe we should go walking together ... unless you would rather get another dog?'

Judith opened her mouth to reply, but the telephone chose that moment to ring and she picked it up and listened intently, astonished at what the caller at the other end was saying to her.

'But he's here beside me. Shouldn't you be saying all this to him?' She glanced up at Rory, who was leaning forward, hand outstretched expectantly. 'Oh, I see. Yes, of course, but I still think ... No? All right, but he's not going to be too pleased . . . What? Well, yes, but . . . OK, Ben, I'll tell him. Take care.'

She put the receiver down and saw disbelief flood Rory's face.

'That was Ben? My son? Why didn't you let me speak to him?'

'Because,' Judith said, 'he asked me

specifically not to put you on.'

'What's happened? Is he ill? Hurt? Why didn't he want to speak to me, Judith?'

'He said he didn't want you to spoil his lovely day,' Judith said, repeating what Ben had told her to say. 'He said that he couldn't face having you shout at him down the phone and that by the time he got to see you, you might have calmed down.'

'For God's sake, Judith, what's happened?'

'Ben got married this morning,' she said and saw his face lose colour and turn an angry shade of grey.

'Damn him! After all I told him!' Rory's fist hid the desk and sent a box of paperclips scattering. 'Married?'

'Her name's Penny and they're very much in love.'

'It's that damned girl he's drooled over since he was fifteen. Why the hell couldn't he wait until . . . I'll wring their necks.'

'No you won't, Rory Telford!' It was

Sarah's voice from the door. 'You'll grow up and welcome the girl into your family. Ben's a man and I'd say he knows his mind a damned sight better than his father does.'

Rory gave her a searing look. 'He'll regret it and then where will we be?' he said.

'If he does regret it, then he'll cope with it and live with the consequences just like everybody else. And I daresay it won't be the only mistake he'll make in his life.'

'Sarah's right, Rory,' Judith said and he gave her a furious look before storming out of the room, muttering something about women always knowing best.

17

'So you see, Dad, it's not nearly as bad as you thought!' Ben and his new bride, Penny, were sitting side by side, hand in hand, in Sarah's sitting-room. They looked incredibly young, wide-eyed and so much in love. Judith watched and waited, with them, for Rory's response and much-needed blessing.

It was Christmas Day and Sarah had invited everyone for lunch, hoping the occasion would diffuse any remaining aggro between father and son.

'Are you really sure this is what you want?' Rory lifted his head from his hands and fixed them with a look that was hard to ignore. 'Studying and working in a restaurant? I can't see you coping, quite honestly.'

'Dr Telford,' said Penny, a little breathlessly, 'it's all we've ever wanted, from the day we met.'

The young couple had been together as friends and love-birds for three years. They had everything in common, including their ambitions for the future. A restaurant with Ben doing the cooking and Penny taking care of the management side of things.

Penny came from a family of restaurateurs. It was how they got together in the first place. Already, her father and her uncles were training Ben to be a sous-chef in their hotel in Hexham. But the good thing was that they were also insisting that he should continue with his university studies at Newcastle, alongside Penny. By the time the two young people were thirty, they could well own their own restaurant.

'Well,' Sarah breathed out a long sigh and slapped her thighs as she got to her feet, a pleased nod in Judith's direction. 'I'm glad that's settled.'

'Hey, whoa, there,' Rory objected, hands in the air. 'I don't seem to have had any say in this . . . '

'Dad, whatever you say now . . . ' Ben shrugged his shoulders. 'Well, it's too late. I know you think I'm a fool, but maybe you'll have to admit you were wrong some day.'

'I just don't agree,' Rory said. 'You should have waited.'

'Rory Telford, if you can't see that Ben and Penny were not only made for each other, but deadly serious, then you're a bigger fool than I took you for,' Sarah snapped out, but then she was smiling again immediately. 'Now, who's for some hot rum punch? I've made it extra strong this year. Thought we'd all need fortifying, and I was right.'

'Well, Dad?' Ben glanced pensively at Judith, then returned his attention to his father.

'All right, all right! I can see I'm overruled.' Rory said. 'It'll just take some time to adjust to the fact that I'm the father of a married man.'

'Hallelujah!' Sarah gasped and headed for the kitchen and the rum punch.

Once the atmosphere had relaxed

somewhat, thanks to the soothing punch, which was not only full of rum, but laced heavily with spices, Sarah put on some Christmas music. Then she clapped her hands and suggested that they all open their presents, which were piled beneath the branches of her twinkling Christmas tree.

Sarah and Judith had conferred over what to do about the young newlyweds, so there was a variety of useful household things there to get them started, since they were to be living in a small furnished flat not far from the university campus. Rory eyed the presents from the women and looked morose.

'You've been very generous,' he said to Judith as they sat together on the sofa watching Ben and Penny exclaim with pleasure over their gifts. 'After all, they're not your kids.'

Judith shrugged. 'It is Christmas after all.'

'But you hardly know Ben . . . and Penny not at all.'

'No, but they're the closest I have to a family at the moment,' she said, thinking enviously of her parents with her brother and his family, celebrating Christmas in Australia.

Rory looked thoughtful and his eyes misted over. 'I'd forgotten what it was like, Judith, to have a family. Since Ben's mother died I haven't known how to celebrate Christmas — or anything else, for that matter. At first, you know, I couldn't . . . it wasn't the same without Laura.'

'Yes, I can understand how difficult it must have been.'

'Then I just let it pass, pretending it didn't exist. I became anaesthetised, I suppose. Today, thanks to Sarah . . . and to you, Judith, I feel as if I've got my life back.'

'I'm glad to hear that,' Judith said.

'We are like a family, aren't we?' Ben grinned boyishly and hugged Penny.

'Pretty much, I suppose,' said his father, nodding.

Judith stared into the flames of the

roaring fire that was sending sparks up the chimney. She breathed in the wood smoke, the sweet and spicy smell of the punch and the musky cologne of the man sitting next to her. It was a heady mixture and now the mouth-watering aroma of roast turkey and trimmings wafted through from the kitchen.

She didn't see Rory's hand move, but suddenly his fingers were entwined with hers, cool and firm, sending a ripple of pleasure through her.

'Judith, I was pretty horrible to you at first because . . . well, because what I felt for you deep down kind of took me by surprise. It was so out of the blue, having such deep feelings again for a woman. It sent me straight into shock. I never thought I'd feel like that again. Now . . . '

'Now?'

He shook his head, released her hand and got to his feet. She waited, wondering why he was looking so grim, why he shoved his fists in his pockets like that, with an expression of chagrin.

'I've been such a damned fool,' he announced. 'And now you'll never forgive me.'

'What?'

'I've been so preoccupied, what with one thing and the other and I thought . . . well, it doesn't matter what I thought. I was wrong to think it and . . . ah, God, I'm babbling like old Fred, aren't I?'

'Well, just a bit,' Judith's smile was tight; she didn't know how to take him.

'What on earth is wrong, Rory?' Sarah said as she came into the room carrying more punch and a platter of tiny smoked salmon and caviar canapés.

'Presents!' Rory said, putting feeling into that one word. 'I didn't think . . . I mean, I never . . . '

'No, Rory, you never did think of presents.'

'I've got mine,' Ben piped up, grinning from ear to ear and his father frowned deeply. 'We're friends again, Dad. I couldn't ask for better than that and, well, Penny's my present to you.

She's going to be the best daughter-in-law in the world.'

'That's quite a responsibility.' Penny laughed, her eyebrows shooting up into her hairline. 'I'd better make a start right now.'

She squeezed Ben's hand, then risked planting a kiss on her new father-in-law's cheek. Rory looked embarrassed for a brief moment, then he smiled and the light came back into his eyes.

'I think you might be right, Ben.' He laughed, then turned his gaze on Sarah. 'As for you, Sarah, I know you're looking for a buyer for this place, so how about selling it to me, eh?'

'You always said it was too big for you!' Sarah reminded him, but her eyes were shining enthusiastically.

'I've changed my mind. Besides, if I don't buy the house I'll have to look for another surgery, because the cottage is going to belong to the chef here and his missus.'

'Oh, Dad! That's pretty cool.'

'Oh, Dr Telford, how marvellous!

Thank you so much.' And Rory received a second kiss from his new daughter-in-law.

Oh, dear, thought Judith, her heart sinking. There goes my new home already. There didn't seem to be a place for her in Rory's life after all. Well, she couldn't hang around on the off chance that things could change. She certainly couldn't stay on as his assistant now. That would be like rubbing salt into an open wound.

18

'Judith . . . I . . . ' Rory was addressing her, his eyes deeply troubled and she prepared herself for the worst, though she could have thought of a better time and place to deliver the bad news.

He opened his mouth again, but was interrupted by a banging on the front door. Sarah, who had rushed back into the kitchen to baste the turkey, shouted for Rory to see who was there.

There was a muttered conversation between two male voices, then the door closed and footsteps returned to the sitting-room. Rory came in, bearing a large cardboard box that was a bit dirty and tattered. Behind him, looking uneasy, but scrubbed as clean as a choirboy, was the old tramp, Fred.

'Sarah!' Rory called out and Sarah came running, drying her hands on her apron. 'We can find enough turkey for

Fred here, can't we?'

Sarah blinked, gave Fred the once over with her discerning eye and discovered with surprise, as Judith had, that the man looked impeccably clean for once. She picked up a glass of hot punch and thrust it at him.

'No problem,' she said, giving him a warm smile.

'That's really big of ye, missus,' Fred said, sipping the punch with suspicious care. 'Aye, begod, this is a drop of good stuff.'

'Happy Christmas, Fred,' Judith said, touching his arm and seeing the pleasure in the lined face as he noticed her for the first time.

'Ah, tis you, missus! Tis grand to see you this mornin'. See, I's wearing that there woolly ye gave me, and comfy it is too.'

He patted his chest and she saw that underneath his shabby tweed jacket, he was wearing the chunky sweater she had given him only yesterday when he had called by her caravan to report that he was back and 'feeling as fit as a lop again'.

'And them old thermal vests o' yourn, doctor, are almost as warm as the Evening Chronicle.'

'Bang goes the theory that I'm a hardy individual,' Rory complained with a wry smile.

Judith tried to laugh with the others, but she was finding it difficult to be light-hearted and was afraid she would not get through the rest of the day's festivities without it showing. Perhaps it might be wise to make her excuses now and save face, she thought, but as she struggled to come up with a plausible reason for leaving before she'd even had her Christmas lunch, fate stepped in to stop her.

'What's in the box, Dad?' Ben asked and his father put the carton down on the floor.

'Well, this is something I hadn't entirely planned, but Fred has just solved the problem of a present for Judith here.'

'For me? Oh, I don't need presents . . . ' Judith stuttered out the words, choking on the tightness that had come into her throat.

'Yes you do and, believe it or not, this was exactly what I was going to give you, only there was a hitch and things went wrong at the last minute. Sorry it's not gift wrapped.'

'Really, I can't imagine . . . ' Judith peered into the box as Rory pulled back a tattered old blanket. 'Oh! Oh, my goodness!'

'He's probably not as handsome as dear old Bertie,' Rory said softly as he lifted out the tiny black and white puppy and handed it to her. 'But I bet you'll fall in love with him anyway.'

Judith's eyes filled with tears as she cradled the young Border collie in her arms, feeling the silky softness of its fragile body, and giving herself up completely to the pink licking tongue.

Everyone crowded around, cooing at the pup as if it was a new baby, and the little dog was enjoying the attention with relish.

'Old Mrs Harris, down in the village. Her dog had three pups a few weeks ago. She kept one, sold one to some passing tourist, and promised the third to me. Only the little beggar wandered off, didn't he? Fred here's been helping me look for him.'

'Didn't have to look too far,' Fred told them. 'I woke up this mornin' in me shack, and there he was sittin' laughing at me. Cute little fella, ain't he? Must have found a hole to creep through.'

'He's wonderful, but I don't know if I can keep him,' Judith said sadly and Rory gave her a questioning look. 'Well, if I'm to find somewhere else to live, it could be difficult . . . '

Rory stared at her for a long while, then his eyes narrowed. He passed the puppy to Sarah and, taking Judith by the arm, led her outside into the garden where the winter sunshine was glistening on the frosty ground.

'The dog can stay here with me,' he

said, watching her closely, and she wasn't at all sure what to make of his remark. 'At least, that's what I was hoping.'

'Hoping? Rory, you've got me all confused. I really don't know where I stand. First you let me rent your cottage from you, then you let it drop that you're giving the cottage to your son and his wife, so . . . Well, where does that leave me?'

'Judith, hasn't it dawned on you?'

'Hasn't what dawned on me?'

'That I'm deeply in love with you and . . . '

'In love with me? Well, you have a strange way of going about things, that's all I can say.'

'And I'm asking you to stay on with me — you and your dog — in this house . . . '

'But Rory . . . '

'Judith, I'm asking you to marry me, dammit.'

'Oh!' She licked her dry lips and swallowed with difficulty. 'Oh, I see. I thought . . . well, it doesn't matter what I thought. I was wrong.'

There was a shout from the open door behind them. 'Judith, for goodness sake,' Sarah grinned knowingly. 'Tell him you'll marry him and come back inside so we can celebrate.'

'Well, Judith?' Rory took her in his arms and held her tightly.

'Well . . . ' she hesitated and saw a look of trepidation creep into his dark eyes. 'I did think that people who were in love spent a little more time together before contemplating marriage.'

'Aye, your right, of course. I'm rushing you, but we have known one another for a few months and . . . well, all right. If it's romance you want, you shall have it, but I warn you, Judith . . . I'm sorely out of practice.'

'You could start now and save some time.'

His kiss was long and deep, draining her of any resistance.

'I hope that came up to scratch,' he said breathlessly as he lifted his head and Judith wasn't sure that she could cope with that much passion in one single kiss. She might have responded in kind, had they been alone, but they were being watched.

'That'll do for now,' she said shakily.

'And you'll think about it, will you? Marrying me, I mean.'

'What a silly question, Rory. Of course I will.'

There was a blip of uneasy silence as he regarded her with lowered lids. 'Think about it? Or marry me?'

'Both,' she said, stroking his taught cheek and seeing her future unroll before her eyes. 'Now, I think we'd better go back inside.'

'Not until I've kissed you again — just to prove to myself that the first kiss was real,' he said, his mouth covering hers and his kiss warming her to the very depths of her being.

There was a loud cheer from inside the house where everybody had been watching and listening through opened windows.

'Wow!' Ben whooped and vigorously punched the air. 'Sarah, break out the champagne! Dad's finally done it!'

THE END

Other titles in the
Linford Romance Library:

IN A WELSH VALLEY

Catriona McCuaig

When Ruth Greene's cousin Dora has to go into hospital, Ruth's family rallies round by going to look after the grocery shop she runs in her Welsh mining village in Carmarthenshire. This gives them a respite from the London blitz, but other dangers and excitements await them in their temporary home. Young Basil gets into mischief, while their daughter, Marina, falls in love for the first time. But can her wartime love endure?

MILLION DOLLAR DREAM

Joanna Hunt

Giorgi had secretly adored Rafe all her life, but he was madly in love with — and destined to marry — her sister, Anna. But when Anna died, their fathers' dream to unite the two families and their wineries was thwarted . . . Will Giorgi marry Rafe, give up her city restaurant and return to the Australian Sunset company as his wife, knowing he doesn't love her? Or will she retain her independence, and deny any chance she may have had of happiness with him?

A COUNTRY MOUSE

Fenella Miller

Emily Gibson is a spirited young woman who wishes to make her own way in life. She has been looking after her family since her father died, but with mounting debts something must be done. Deciding that she must marry for money, she writes to ask her estranged grandfather, the Earl of Westerham, to put forward an appropriate suitor. But he selects her cousin — and he's the last person Emily would have chosen. Can love blossom in such circumstances?